Alexis blushed, felt her face flame

Didn't Dan know his grin was lethal? That he really had to keep it to himself? She quickly turned her head and scooped the baby from her play mat. "Time to go for a nice long walk, sweetheart."

"I've got a little time." Dan followed her to the door. "I thought I'd join you."

That was the last thing Alexis wanted— Dan with her while she was trying to forget him. But she couldn't say that. "Sure," said Alexis, "you can push the stroller."

"Great." He leaned over Michelle. "Want Daddy to push your carriage, baby?"

Michelle's eyes drifted closed, and Dan's carefree laughter floated in the air. A musical sound that made Alexis smile.

"The ladies in my life sure know how to take me down a peg."

Boston's star quarterback could laugh at himself—a nice trait. It seemed there was a whole lot more to Dan Delito that Alexis had yet to discover.

Dear Reader,

One of the perks of writing is the research. I learn new things and for *Quarterback Daddy,* I finally learned how to play football. Yes, football. I know it's hard to believe that, although I'm the wife of a dedicated NY Giants fan and the mother of three grown sons, I never paid attention to the battle on the gridiron. My excuse is that my kids were into baseball. I spent years watching Little League games—and reading a romance novel between innings.

Football is complicated. The vocabulary is extensive enough to require its own dictionary. To the untutored eye, the players appear to fall over themselves in a messy pile. I watched games on television, subscribed to *Sports Illustrated* and bought one of those *Dummies* books. I memorized the positions and the vocabulary, and learned who certain key players were. It was worth the effort.

Quarterback Dan Delito had it all. Then his wife died and nothing matters to him after losing her. But his world is turned upside down by Alexis Brown and her baby niece. How she helps him reengage in the game of life was so fun to write.

I'd love to hear from readers. Please e-mail me at Linda@Linda-Barrett.com or write to me at P.O. Box 841934, Houston, TX 77284-1934.

Happy reading!

Linda Barrett

Quarterback Daddy
Linda Barrett

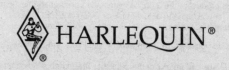

TORONTO • NEW YORK • LONDON
AMSTERDAM • PARIS • SYDNEY • HAMBURG
STOCKHOLM • ATHENS • TOKYO • MILAN • MADRID
PRAGUE • WARSAW • BUDAPEST • AUCKLAND

Recycling programs
for this product may
not exist in your area.

ISBN-13: 978-0-373-78364-9

QUARTERBACK DADDY

www.eHarlequin.com

Printed in U.S.A.

ABOUT THE AUTHOR

Linda has been writing for pleasure all her adult life, but targeted a professional career when she moved to Houston more than ten years ago. There she joined a local chapter of the Romance Writers of America and attended so many workshops and seminars, "I could have had a master's degree by now," she says. Five years later, in 2001, Harlequin Superromance published her debut novel, *Love, Money and Amanda Shaw*. When not writing, the mother of three grown sons ("all hero material like their dad") helps develop programs for a social service agency that works with the homeless.

Books by Linda Barrett

To Elizabeth and Alexis, who always want a story time with Grandma. To Aaron, who never turns down a trip to the bookstore. And to Baby Jacob Ethan, who will soon discover the pleasure of a good book.

It doesn't get better than this for a storytelling Grandma!

CHAPTER ONE

THE BOSTON GLOBE
Friday, July 6
MURDER–SUICIDE ENDS WITH BABY BORN IN AMBULANCE
Sherri Brown, 25, and nine months pregnant, was shot and left for dead last evening in front of her sister's apartment building in the Leather District. The assailant then turned the gun on himself and died at the scene. Ms. Brown succumbed in the ambulance, where her child was delivered by emergency cesarian section. Her sister, Alexis Brown, was with her. Preliminary investigation revealed the gunman to be a former boyfriend of the victim.

THREE MONTHS AFTER THE tragedy, Alexis Brown deliberately removed the news clipping from her kitchen message board and placed it in an envelope for safekeeping. Reading wasn't necessary; she'd memorized the article. The headline, however, still had the power to suck the air out of her. Even now, as she handled the clipping, her pulse fluttered when memories of that night tortured her like scenes from a well-made horror movie.

She remembered running downstairs after Sherri to return a child-care book her sister had forgotten to take. Arriving just in time to watch a man shoot himself, and to see Sherri lying on the sidewalk. Calling 9-1-1 on her cell phone. Watching the doctor and the EMT deliver the baby. Holding Sherri's hand, straining to hear her last words, whispered directly into Alexis's ear.

She shivered head to toe, her stomach cramping as she thought about the police report, the result of a first-rate investigation. She'd learned more than she'd really wanted to know.

Clasping a pen, she wrote Michelle's name on the envelope, sealed it and filed the newspaper article with the baby's other legal papers in the bottom drawer of her desk. When her niece grew up, she'd be entitled to read it.

When her niece grew up... Alexis tiptoed to the crib in the bedroom where Michelle napped peacefully, her little forehead unlined, her breathing strong and even. Beautiful, sweet and innocent. Exactly the way a baby should be, and the way Alexis had vowed this baby's life would be. She wouldn't fail Michelle the way she'd failed Michelle's mom.

Leaving the bedroom quietly, Alexis returned to her desk in the main area of her apartment, a condo conversion. She loved the place, but she'd have to sell it, and the market was awful. Prices were falling in the depressed economy, and she'd be lucky to break even.

Money. Everything always came down to money.

She reached for the phone, hoping Roz would be available to brainstorm. Only a few years older than Alexis, the baby's social worker had been supportive from Day One, and Alexis trusted her as much as she could trust anybody.

With Roz's cheery hello, Alexis sighed in relief. "How are you feeling about problem solving today?"

"Diaper rash or teething?"

"If only. I need a miracle, Roz, like hitting the day-care lottery."

"Ouch. That's a tough one."

"You said it. Every place I visited downtown is way out of my reach. I can't afford any of them, and I don't qualify for reduced fees despite earning peanuts." She felt panic start to build inside her. "I've got to return to work on the twenty-ninth. That's only three weeks away!"

"Easy, Alexis," Roz soothed. "Easy. I'm listening."

"I know, but I'm stuck, Roz. Between the student loans and the mortgage, I don't have a lot of savings. I've only been working for two years. My credit card is maxed out with all the baby stuff and…and…my normal expenses."

"I'm listening to your every word, Alexis, but I didn't hear you mention the biggest culprit of all, and certainly not a 'normal' expense. As usual, you're being too hard on yourself."

Alexis remained silent, fighting tears.

"Funeral costs are high," Roz continued, "and you've shouldered that alone."

"Did I have a choice?" Alexis whispered, her throat hurting. "Sherri would still be lying in the morgue if I'd depended on Cal and Peggy. You know how 'parental' they are." She swallowed her sarcasm with a deep breath and regained her balance.

"I know all about them, and sadly, what you say is true," said Roz. She sighed deeply, so deeply that Alexis heard the woman's exhalation through the phone.

"Ironically, your sister would have qualified for financial aid, but you don't. You're off work right now, however, so I can give you vouchers for neighborhood food pantries…"

"Food pantries? Roz, I'm not *homeless*." She heard the horror in her voice. Even her family had never resorted to food pantries.

"Right," said Roz. "And we're trying to prevent that."

Stay calm. Her palms began to sweat. "I can earn a living for Michelle and me. I worked hard to get through college, then law school…."

"I know that. You've impressed me from the first time we met, but I've got to speak honestly here," said Roz. "You've got temporary custody of Michelle until it's finalized in the courts. You are the baby's closest and, in my opinion, most capable relative. But if you think you can't handle the responsibility right now, we could go the foster route just until—"

"No! Please, no foster care. I'll handle it. I'll even use the food vouchers. And—and I'll put the condo on the market. Today. The hell with the financial loss."

Damn! She shouldn't have called Roz after all. Give Michelle up? Never!

The baby already recognized her. She knew Alexis's step, her touch. Since Michelle had started smiling a week ago, they'd laughed and played silly games all day long. They were a team. They loved each other. Michelle's home was with Alexis. Period. In a few more months, Alexis would become Michelle's legal mom. End of story.

Roz was still talking and Alexis tuned in again.

"There's one other possibility," said the woman. "I wonder… Alexis, when you packed up your sister's apartment, did you go through her clothes, look in her pockets? Maybe letters, notes, phone messages?"

Alexis had returned to Sherri's place two days after Michelle's birth, once the police had searched for evidence and removed the yellow tape. Her sister's belongings had been scattered about in her usual haphazard style.

"I bagged her clothes for donations, emptied drawers. Took whatever baby clothes and items she'd bought. What are you getting at?"

"It takes two people to make a baby, kiddo. Michelle's father—"

"Did you find out who he is?" Alexis interrupted, her throat tight once more, her heart beating in double time.

"No, I didn't," replied Roz slowly. "I was hoping you might have discovered a clue, something in Sherri's apartment maybe. DNA ruled out the guy who killed her. We know that much."

The negative DNA results left the path open

to someone else, someone Alexis had been able to target. She was not ready, however, to share that information. So she took a deep breath and lied to her closest ally.

"I didn't find anything, Roz. Nothing. *Nada.* I don't know any more than you do."

Protecting the baby was and would always be her highest priority. She would initiate a thorough investigation of the baby's possible father on her own before she made her next move. She had two weeks to figure it all out, before she had to start considering bankruptcy to eliminate some of her debt. Just like her own dysfunctional parents had done recently. The irony didn't escape her.

DAN DELITO, STARTING quarterback for the New England Patriots, slouched in his favorite club chair, staring at the wallet-size picture of Kim that he carried with him at all times. Tonight would have been their ninth anniversary but for the breast cancer that had consumed her almost two years ago. He stroked a shaking finger across her beautiful face and down her long dark hair, wavy and soft. *Oh, baby, baby…I miss you so much.* It was so unfair. To her. To him. His gentle, loving wife had deserved better than virulent cancer cells and toxic chemo.

She'd deserved a long life, with children and family and good times. He would have given her twelve kids if she'd said the word. Whatever she'd wanted, she could have had.

He eyed the bottle of single-malt Scotch on the table next to him. It was half-gone, and his empty glass stood waiting for a refill. No one could say he was a cheap drunk, that's for sure. He grabbed the bottle and poured. The smooth amber liquid would make the pain go away.

"Danny? You didn't hear the bell, so we let ourselves...Danny! What are you doing? Dear God, not again!"

He turned his head, glass to his lips. His folks. He took a swallow. "Come on in. Grab a couple of glasses and join me. It's my anniversary, and we have to toast Kim. My Kimmy."

He took another sip, watched his parents put down aluminum-foil-wrapped packages. The aroma from them was delicious, homemade from his parents' Italian deli, but his stomach suddenly rebelled. "Be right back."

Ten minutes later, he found his folks in the kitchen, warming up some braciole. The marinated steak was one of his favorites. His mom served it in spaghetti sauce with a salad and warm bread on the side. He wanted it, but his insides threatened another revolt.

"I need some air." He opened the back door and stepped onto the patio of his four-story town house. Kim had loved this place, and she'd turned it into a real home for them. Her presence lingered in every room, and that made him feel good.

He inhaled the crisp autumn air. Football weather. The best time of the year. Goose bumps popped out all over his body as he thought of this weekend's home game. Another deep breath cleared his head, settled his stomach.

He sensed a big shadow behind him. His dad.

"You can't go on like this, son."

"I'm fine, Dad. Don't worry. It's because of the anniversary, that's all."

"And what was the excuse last week?" Nicky Delito wasn't letting go.

"Last week, I knew it was coming," said Dan. "Come on, Dad, we're tied for the best record in the league. What more do you want?"

His dad equaled him in size, but suddenly loomed larger than ten linebackers, as he had when Dan was a kid.

"What more do I want?" Nicky bellowed. "I want a sober son again. I want your mother to stop crying over you. Praying on her knees every single night. Your brother…your sister… the kids. You're always the topic of conversation and it's enough. You hear me, Danny-boy? I want a son I can count on. That's what I want!"

"Nicky, stop yelling." His mom stood in the doorway to the patio. Danny waved to her, but then addressed his father.

"You can count on me, Dad. On the weekends, on the field. I haven't let the team down yet, and I don't intend to. My coaches, the management—everyone's happy with our performance so far, and we have a home game this Sunday."

Nicky raised both arms up in the air and let them fall to his sides. He looked at his wife. "He doesn't get it. Who gives a damn about a football game when his life's a mess?"

"If I didn't care about the game, Dad, I'd drink all the time. Now, I only drink in the middle of the week." He clapped his dad on the shoulder. "Don't worry. I can handle being a part-time drinker."

"Maybe you should join a twelve-step program," said Rita Delito.

"Are you kidding, Ma? Those programs are for *real* alcoholics."

His parents stared at him.

"What?"

Their silence continued.

"Oh, come on. I can stop whenever I want to."

"Prove it." His dad wasted no time. "No more drinking at all. Not even midweek."

His mom looked so hopeful, her brown eyes wide and shining up at him. God, he loved these two people.

"Okay. I won't have another drink for the next seven days."

"It's a start," said Rita.

"I'm going to empty the liquor cabinet when we leave tonight," Nicky said. "Just to make sure."

Dan's mind raced, picturing the rest of the house. Yeah, he'd brought a bottle to his bedroom last week.

"Okay."

"And I'll check out the rest of the place," Nicky added.

"No," Dan replied quickly.

His dad was like that. Always knew what was going on in his kids' heads, in their lives. Dan, Joe, Theresa—none of them ever got away with anything when they were small, and it seemed they wouldn't as adults, either. Not even the quarterback for the New England Patriots.

"No?" repeated Nick softly. "I've done some research, Danny. That's what a twelve-step sponsor would do with you. Together, you'd clean out the house. Your brother and I, we're going to act like your sponsors."

"No. You're not." He gulped for air. A face-off with his dad was an extraordinary event, but now he looked Nicky straight in the eye. "I'm over twenty-one, Dad. I can handle it."

Stalemate. Until his mom's soft voice interrupted. "What would Kim say, Danny, if she saw you like this?"

Mothers. He grabbed the back of a chair with two hands. "If I could have her with me again," he replied, his Adam's apple bobbing, "I'd give up everything. The bottles. The touchdowns. The career. The house. The money. Nothing I've got is worth a damn thing without her."

Fighting the tears behind his eyes, he turned around, walked past his mother and into the house, opened the fridge and took out a longneck. "Anyone else?"

"There's no talking to him," said Nicky.

Rita sighed and banged a plate onto the table. "At least eat first. Today is only Tuesday. Do we have to come back tomorrow?"

ORDINARILY, ALEXIS WOULDN'T have connected the crisp cool days and blazing autumn colors of New England with perfect football weather. In fact, she wouldn't have noted the football season at all. Alexis was not a fan of the game, a game where grown men tried to kill their opponents and themselves. During the three months since Michelle's birth, however, she'd made it her business to read the sports pages every day and track the progress of the New England Patriots. She'd focused mainly on one particular player: Dan Delito, starting QB and captain of the team. From what she read, the man obviously knew his business, worked hard and was leading his team in a winning season.

On Wednesday, two mornings after her phone conversation with Roz, Alexis noted the NFL schedule for the following Sunday and then headed toward her bedroom, where it sounded as though Michelle had awakened from her nap. As soon as the baby saw her, she flashed her magical baby grin, and Alexis's heart melted one more time. Her love for this child constantly astounded her. In the beginning, after Michelle was born, Alexis had had no idea how awesome motherhood would be.

She changed Michelle's diaper and returned to the living room that had morphed into an infant's playground. "I bet you're hungry, petunia, aren't you? You're always hungry."

Michelle's brown eyes opened wide and she waved her arms with excitement. Alexis was just as excited. She would swear the baby was trying to talk to her. She kept up a stream of patter while she warmed the bottle of formula, all the while thinking about the excursion she'd planned for them that afternoon.

A visit to *Michelle's father.* She could no longer ignore Dan Delito's existence.

After racking her brain for other solutions, she was back to where she'd started. Quitting her job was not an option; she needed an income. But on her salary, she couldn't afford proper day care. Her parents certainly weren't an option, not with her father still hitting the bottle. So, she'd either lose Michelle to the foster care system, or she could split custody of the baby with Dan Delito. Money was certainly not a problem for him! She now had less than three weeks to work it out so she could return to her job.

Alexis was almost a hundred percent sure Delito was the dad. Although her sister had never spoken about the father of her child, she'd had no reason to lie in the ambulance. Could she have realized, even as she lay dying, that Alexis would need the financial and emotional support of a partner, just as Alexis would have been a support for Sherri? Was that the reason her sister had whispered Dan's name at the very end? Sherri had made foolish choices in her life, but there was nothing wrong with her IQ.

And then there was the file of year-old newspaper clippings she'd found in Sherri's apartment. Articles from the sports pages, mostly football, mostly Patriots, always Dan Delito's name circled every time it appeared.

She missed her sister, her pretty sister with the dazzling smile. Sometimes Alexis's guilt choked her to the point of nausea. Alexis was older. She should have looked out for Sherri better. But Sherri could disappear like a wisp of smoke. She'd go off with girlfriends, with men, or follow her favorite teams. First with Alexis's heavy schedule at school and her many part-time jobs, and then with her busy days at the D.A.'s office, she'd easily lost track of her sister's activities.

Excuses, excuses. Remorse pierced her again, and her lips trembled. "I'm going to take such good care of you, sweetheart," she whispered to the baby. "And I'll make sure that daddy of yours is superterrific before I leave you with him for even an hour."

THAT SAME WEDNESDAY afternoon, Dan Delito was watching Colts footage at home in his Beacon Hill neighborhood. The seventh game of the season would be played this Sunday at Gillette Stadium, the Patriots' turf outside the city. They had a sold-out crowd of loyal fans, and now Dan sat forward in his leather club chair, studying the opposition's habits, their strengths, their weaknesses. Where the possibilities lay. He thought about the guys on his own team, and how they stacked up against their counterparts.

He drained his bottle of beer and threw the empty in the trash can with its brothers. Beer wasn't like *real* alcohol; Kim had never minded him downing a beer. Of course, she'd never seen him drink a whole six-pack in an afternoon.

He studied the screen again. Football. The one thing he could count on. If it weren't for the game, he'd have nothing to make him get up in the morning. But now, Peyton Manning looked blurry. Geez! How fast was the Colts' QB running? And why was he carrying the ball this time instead of handing it off? Maybe…maybe the guy wasn't Manning? It wasn't. The Colts' receiver was heading for the end zone with no one blocking him. Dan made a mental note for his linebackers, cornerbacks and safeties. New England couldn't allow that.

His head began to pound, but he picked up the remote, rewound the tape and started watching from the beginning. Now he was so focused, he chose to ignore the ringing doorbell. It chimed a second time, and he made an annoyed gesture with his hand as though brushing off an insect. It couldn't be anyone important. Both his immediate and extended families led busy lives in the middle of the day. They all worked hard. Weekends, of course, were different when Danny played. Then, the entire clan showed up at the stadium or watched the away games on television, usually at his parents' house. The sport was definitely a family activity.

When the doorbell rang a third time, Danny cursed out loud, hoisted himself from the chair and clambered down the mahogany staircase to the front door. He pulled it hard.

"What?" he barked from the threshold.

His visitor had already left, however, and was ten feet from his town house, her long hair bouncing against her back just below her shoulders. Thick, dark hair. Wavy hair.

Time stopped, and he froze. He stared until she started to disappear. Then Dan stepped farther outside, where the bright sun blinded him and ratcheted up his headache to new levels of pain. He clutched the wrought-iron railing with one hand, while the other shaded his eyes enough so he could squint after the woman.

Kim's dark hair, her beautiful hair, bounced

just like that once…. The same straight posture, the slender body and those long shapely legs below the skirt…

He couldn't breathe. Was God giving them another chance? Or was he hallucinating? Was this the d.t.'s?

"Hello," he called.

She turned her head, her smile grew and she held her index finger up. "Hang on a sec."

Hell, yes! He'd hang on for hours if she asked. That smile. Pure sunshine. From a distance, he could only guess her eyes were dark as Kimmy's were. He continued to watch her, then understood the delay. She was pushing a baby stroller, leaning over it and talking at the same time.

He walked toward her, every step reverberating through his body, his head ready to explode. Pain didn't matter. He wasn't going to miss this chance.

"You need some help?" he asked as he came abreast of her, memorizing every nuance. Not Kim. These eyes were hazel. This woman was a bit taller…but he found these small differences easy to ignore.

She looked up then and stepped back. Whatever friendliness he'd thought he'd seen evaporated. Her eyes accused him as if she had the right.

"Ugh! Your breath. It stinks…stinks from… beer. Well, I see this visit was a mistake. Just get away from me, and get far away from the baby."

He didn't need a public scene. Besides, she didn't sound like Kim. His Kim would never have made such a disgusted face at him. Of course, she'd have had no reason. He never drank in the old days. But it felt damn good now.

He opened his arms wide. "Keep your cool. I'm leaving. No harm, no foul." He turned to go and heard her voice again.

"You are Dan Delito, aren't you?"

Another groupie. He didn't need this. Or… maybe he did. The girls came in handy after a game, when the guys were high off a win or needed consolation after a loss. For a little while, anyway, Dan could forget about cancer and Kim's ordeal. He could forget about feeling lost himself.

Keeping his distance, he said, "And what if I am?"

"Is that a yes or a no?" she asked, stepping in front of the baby stroller, her head tilted back to meet his gaze.

He studied her at length, all heavenly ideas forgotten. No hallucinations. No miracles. No second chances. The woman was not like Kim at all. "What are you, some kind of lawyer?"

"Touchdown. So, answer the question."

This barracuda could have chewed Kim up and spit her out. However, *he* wasn't Kim.

"Who's asking?" he demanded, standing his ground.

For the first time, she hesitated, her gaze traveling from the top of his head down to his running shoes. Finally, she pulled a card from her purse—as well as a stick of gum—and handed both to him. "My name is Alexis Brown."

"I see," he said, studying the card. "The District Attorney's office?" The black print seemed to dance on the white background, but he thought he'd read the words correctly. "What's this all about?" He considered his activities during the last few days and remembered nothing unusual. Of course, he might not be remembering everything….

The woman seemed to have come to a decision. "I'm sorry, Mr. Delito. I see I've made a mistake. Why don't we both forget about this visit? You can go back inside and…and do whatever it is a player does in the afternoon, and I'll get out of your way."

She put her hand out to retrieve her business card, but his reflexes were still quick, and he whipped it behind his back. "Not so fast."

Her eyebrows hit her hairline. "Yes, fast. I'm

outta here, right now." But her gaze lingered on him for a moment, then she shrugged. "I bet you'll never remember this conversation anyway…you'll think it was a vague dream after you sleep it off." She sighed audibly. "That's the way it works when Jack Daniel's takes over."

She started walking toward the corner, but as she turned away he caught a glimpse of her expressive face, so poignant and soft when she looked at the baby. He heard her mumbling to herself, saw her shaking her head.

He unwrapped the stick of gum and chewed hard. He'd remember the conversation, all right, because he wouldn't forget her resemblance to Kim. Returning to his house, he tucked her card in his wallet.

DISAPPOINTMENT HIT HER with the ferocity of a thunderstorm. Alexis took several deep breaths as she walked the long way home with the baby, realizing for the first time how much she'd been counting on Dan Delito to be the answer to her dilemma. But there was no way she'd relinquish Michelle to a drunk, no matter how handsome or famous or powerful. What a waste.

Had she not done her research, she would have kicked herself. But she had. She'd looked for information about Dan Delito everywhere, scouring the newspapers, the Internet, *Sports Illustrated* and other magazines for comments about him from his teammates. She'd learned he'd been born in the north end of the city, came from a big extended Italian family, graduated from Ohio State, got married shortly afterward. Seven years later, his wife died. He'd been seen at a couple of clubs with different women in the past year, but nothing more remarkable than that. No drunken scenes, no scandals. No nothing.

Since August, a month after Michelle's birth, Alexis had followed the team's progress at training camp and through four preseason games and now through the regular season. She thought she'd done her due diligence.

None of the newspaper articles mentioned a drinking problem. So, somehow, his drinking didn't interfere with his performance on the field.

"Not yet, anyway," she murmured to herself. But it would at some point, just as it had with her father. Among other things, Calvin Brown was a functioning alcoholic who'd lost his business after almost a lifetime of drinking. Dan would lose his career, too. It was a question of when, not if.

She looked into the stroller. "In the end, Michelle, the liquor always wins. It can turn some people into monsters. So no drunken daddy for you. We'll have to think of something else."

In the half hour it took her to walk home and go upstairs, she came up with several work-from-home ideas, but nothing practical. Nothing that paid well from the start. But at least she'd taken some definitive action. A real estate agent was visiting her tomorrow. They'd discuss listing her condo.

A few minutes after she changed Michelle's diaper, her cell phone rang.

"Alexis speaking."

"I'm not an alcoholic. You just caught me at a bad time."

She recognized Delito's voice instantly. "At two in the afternoon? Give me a break. Besides, you don't owe me an explanation. We're done."

"Does law school teach you to make snap decisions?"

"I had evidence and plenty of it."

"And I had extenuating circumstances. My ninth wedding anniversary. It's been a tough week. You might want to consider that before you rush to judgment."

She let out a slow breath, remembering he was a widower. "Point to you, Mr. Delito. I'll reserve judgment—for now." She was surprised he sounded coherent.

"So, what does the D.A.'s office want with me?"

He called because he was worried, but it was an easy question. "Absolutely nothing, Mr. Delito. I came on a personal matter. My business card was all I had on me."

"A personal matter? Want to explain that?"

"I'm sorry, but I don't. I'm also sorry about your wife, but you were in a bad way today, and I'm not ready to chat. I don't know whether to trust you yet."

He disconnected the call.

She stared at the silent mobile, satisfied at having learned something about him. The man had pride. She hoped there was substance behind it.

CHAPTER TWO

"Barracuda" had been a compliment—the woman was a shark. Dan's nostrils flared and his mouth tightened as he fingered her business card in the kitchen of his town house. Not trust him? A fifty-five-man roster trusted his every move. Ten teammates watched him like hawks on the field, not to mention the opposition players checking him out. He hadn't disappointed his men yet, and he wouldn't. The game was the only thing he had left.

Her card said, Alexis Brown, J.D. Well, he had his own lawyers—paid them plenty to read his contracts, monitor stories in the press and keep him out of trouble. Now Andy Romano could do some research, as well. His closest pal when they were growing up, Andy had recently been made a partner in his firm. Talk about trust—they'd take a bullet for each other. He punched in his friend's number.

"I need a favor."

Andy's laugh made Danny laugh. "You're paying me, Danny-boy. It's not a favor. Shoot."

Dan read the information from Alexis's business card. "Find out what you can about her. I don't know why she came to the house, but she had something serious on her mind. She wasn't a groupie and…she had a baby with her."

A long, low whistle came through the phone. "A baby? Danny-boy, suddenly, I'm thinking something not-so-good."

"No way. She's one woman I'd never forget. And I never saw her until today."

"Excellent. I'm breathing again. I'll start with public records right away and get back to you later. It shouldn't take too long. Oh, and I'll be in the stands on Sunday. Think we'll make it through to the you-know-what this year?"

Dan groaned. The Super Bowl. That was the single topic of the football season he avoided. Hated questions about it, so didn't allow his friends or family to even say the *S* word within his hearing. Occasionally they got creative, but he *never* offered a direct answer.

"I take it one contest at a time, my man. One game is all I can concentrate on. But come to the house after the game and bring

Pauline. We have an early kickoff at noon. Plenty of time to party afterward. The whole family will be here."

"Will do."

Dan disconnected and made his way to his home gym in the basement, bypassing the cold beer in the fridge and ignoring his liquor cabinet. He needed a clear head. Alternating the stationary bike with the Bowflex machine, he worked up a sweat, felt the renewed strength in his arms and legs and started to focus on Sunday. Tomorrow he'd be on the field for a practice with the offensive line. The guys would be looking to him and the coaches. He had to be ready. He *would* be ready. No drinking.

When Andy called over an hour later, Dan was out of the shower and back in front of the television, screening footage again.

"What've you got?" asked Dan.

"Basics so far. A hometown girl from Southie. Thirty-one years old. Graduated from Boston University Law two years ago and went right into the D.A.'s office. It took her eight years to get her undergrad degree, so her career started later than usual."

"Married?" asked Dan.

"No record of it."

"What about the kid?"

"I can do some deeper digging tomorrow," Andy said.

"Maybe she was babysitting."

"Maybe, but I don't like the idea of a home visit. You never know when the paparazzi gets wind of something or invents a story from thin air. I don't like it at all." He paused. "Did you smell like a brewery?"

"Maybe a bit." Despite his best efforts, Dan's voice had a sharp edge.

"So, Danny—how's that going?"

"I'm fine. And I don't need another father." He had everything under control.

"I couldn't be Nicky if I tried. But I love you like a brother, Danny, and I care. Pauline cares, too. She worries about you."

Andy and Pauline. Danny and Kim. They used to pal around often together in the old days. Close friends. Trusting friends. They'd shared so much, including the pain of losing Kim.

"Andy?"

"Yeah?"

"Today, when that woman came over…for a minute, I thought she was Kimmy." His voice broke.

"Oh, hell, Danny. I'll be right there."

That's what friends did for friends. Dan was one lucky dude. "Thanks, but don't bother. My folks threatened to return tonight. I'll be fine. In fact, I *am* fine. In the end, she wasn't Kim."

With a heavy heart, he said goodbye and clicked the phone off.

IN HER CONDO THE NEXT DAY, Alexis cringed when she signed the listing papers with the real estate agent.

"I love this place," she said to the young woman with the fat notebook and laptop. "I bought it with my very own money, my very own *hard-earned* money. A good down payment. Lived on a strict budget. And now, I'll be taking a loss on the investment. I can't believe it, but I need to generate cash." She glanced at the baby in the swing.

For the first time in her life, she missed having what she knew other women had—girlfriends. Girlfriends to talk things over with, to ask for advice and give advice in return. In childhood she'd had to watch every word and keep her family life a secret. In those days, she and Sherri had been a twosome, depending solely on each other.

Between her part-time jobs and schoolwork, she'd had no time to cultivate friendships in college. At least, that's what she told herself. She wasn't too good at forming relationships with men, either. She'd had one brief love affair as a student that ended badly—all her fault. She still cringed at the memories. But now, she needed someone to talk to, a friend of either gender. Life was becoming more complicated, not less, and at this moment, she was chatting with a virtual stranger.

"Maybe you could advertise for a roommate," said the real estate agent. "I won't make any money—I'm talking myself out of a listing here—but, frankly, I've known some hard times myself."

Alexis listened and hope soared. "A roommate?" New idea. With other people around, she could really brainstorm. "I'll let you know if anything changes, but in the meantime, list the apartment. And please keep an eye out for an inexpensive rental—if such a thing exists in this city."

After the agent left, she called Roz.

"If I had a regular roommate, a working woman like me, her rent could help me pay for daycare," she told the social worker in a breathless rush.

"That could work, but I'd have to investigate anyone you brought into your home at this point."

That made sense. Roz's job was to protect Michelle. "Well…do you know someone looking for a place to live?" A recommendation from Roz would seal the deal.

"I'd have to think about it. But…Alexis, I want to be up-front with you." The woman's words came slowly. "I'm preparing the foster care paperwork, just in case. The days are flying by, and foster families appreciate a heads-up. I'm sorry."

"Oh, my God, Roz! You can't do that. Michelle loves me, and I love her. She's mine. And besides, transferring her to strangers would be letting Sherri down."

"The baby *is* yours, Alexis. That doesn't change. This is simply a temporary measure until your finances are under control and day care arrangements can be made."

But Alexis's nerve endings jangled, warning bells clanged, and her stomach lurched. This nightmare couldn't be happening. Not to her. Not to Michelle. There were plenty of single parents successfully raising kids by themselves. Was she any less capable? She couldn't believe that, but…but maybe those women received child support or other aid that she didn't have.

She trusted Roz—one of the very few people she did trust—and now the woman had given her something new to worry about.

"Surely, there has to be something available for me," Alexis said.

"I'm so sorry, Alexis, but you already know that day-care assistance is need-based, and your income is too high for us to underwrite you."

The nightmare continued. She had less than three hundred dollars left in the bank, which she'd earmarked for emergencies. Now, a headache took root, pounding harder with each minute that passed. Her legs danced with nervous energy, the way they had when she was a kid. The whole world had been against her then, too. A world of broken promises.

Yes, you can. No, you can't. College? Foolish girl. Who do you think you are?

She usually tried not to look back. But now, she actually stroked her cheek as she hung up the phone, remembering the slaps. The punches. And worse.

With all his money, Dan Delito could solve her problems. He might even want to know he had a child. But did he deserve another chance? She simply didn't know. And she couldn't put Michelle at risk with a drunk.

BY THE THIRD QUARTER OF Sunday's game, the teams were tied at fourteen. They seemed evenly matched to Alexis, with two touchdowns at six points each and good kicks for the points after. From the recesses of her mind, she'd dredged up the little football knowledge she'd stored.

"Delito gets the snap," called the TV announcer, "and is sacked right in the pocket…."

Alexis saw was a bunch of huge guys in a pile and guessed that Dan was on the very bottom. He hadn't had a chance to pass the ball. The fans in the stadium were quiet. Not a good sign.

"Seems like the guy's in trouble, Michelle. Maybe he's not concentrating." Maybe he had a hangover. No, that wasn't a fair assessment. Football was a ferocious contact sport; it was easy to get sacked.

The baby vocalized her agreement, and Alexis leaned down to smother her in kisses, as she did a dozen times a day. The sweet pea loved "talking" with her about any subject and continued babbling now. Alexis had a better time playing with the baby than watching the game.

An hour later, after Dan had been sacked twice more, the two-minute warning sounded. Dan threw a long straight pass to his wide receiver, who ran the ball for almost thirty yards and blasted into the end zone. Touchdown. Patriots' victory.

"And the crowd goes wild…" she murmured, fascinated by the unabashed enthusiasm in the stadium. The fans had lived and breathed each play, their emotions on a rollercoaster ride throughout the afternoon. She understood it intellectually but didn't feel it as though they did. Her own life was filled with rollercoaster emotions based on real issues. Didn't these people have lives of their own? Shouldn't they be pursuing their own goals, rather than someone else's artificial ones on a football field of dreams? It was only a game. A waste of time.

She was about to turn the television off when the cameras focused on the press box and an interview with Dan Delito and Al Tucker, the wide receiver. Helmets off, but they were dressed in their dark blue uniforms with their signature logo—a patriot's face and tricornered hat—on the sleeve. As she studied Delito, she had to admit the quarterback could hold his own in the good looks department. Well-built, certainly. Thick dark hair, a surprisingly straight nose after his long career, and a firm mouth. Handsome, but also rugged with his square jaw and scruffy beard. Man, she'd noticed a load of details, appealing and attractive details.

"It was crunch time today, Dan," said the announcer. "How'd you do it in the end?"

Dan spoke into the microphone. "Like I always do. With the help of my teammates. Al

Tucker was on the mark. He got through the Colts' defensive line—a tough line, by the way. Great work from this guy." He slapped Tucker on the shoulder.

"You got sacked at few times today. How do you feel?"

"Like I got sacked a few times today." Delito grinned at the interviewer, eyes gleaming. "I'll live."

The two players walked off, laughing to each other. Dan, however, sported a slight limp. Being underneath a pile of gladiators must not have been fun, but he hadn't complained.

Alexis stared at the screen for several minutes after the men had disappeared. There was no way Dan Delito had an ounce of alcohol in him today. Not the way he played. Not the way he spoke. And not the way he looked. His eyes had sparkled with humor, he knew exactly what he was doing, and he moved with the smooth grace of the athlete he was.

Maybe she really had caught him at a bad moment because of his anniversary. One indulgence didn't mean he was an addict.

She was going to visit him again.

DAN CALLED HER MONDAY morning, before she could plan the outing.

"Did you watch the game?" No hello. No how-are-you.

"How's the leg?" she asked.

His chuckle was deep and rich, almost musical, and caused shivers to run through her.

"Whaddyaknow? She's a fan."

It was her turn to laugh. "Hmm… Not quite. What I understand about football could be be written on the head of a pin. But I saw enough to reconsider a meeting. I—I might have rushed to judgment the other day."

"Well, I appreciate that," he drawled, his voice now laced with a touch of sarcasm. "So tell me why I should care. What's this 'business' all about?"

Alexis took a deep breath. "I won't discuss it on the phone. It's too private and important. But I'd be happy to meet you in the Common at the Frog Pond, or I could come to your place again. Whatever you'd prefer."

"My lawyer says to stay away from you. He says he found you mentioned in several news articles and you're trouble."

He worked fast. Did he think he needed protection? "Your lawyer? I'm sure I don't even know your lawyer. I'm just a little cog in the D.A.'s wheel."

"A little cog? Not for long, Alexis Brown, not

after graduating law school at the top of the class, not after doing the same in political science at the undergrad level. No, ma'am. I predict you'll score your own touchdowns one day soon."

She hadn't been expecting an investigation. Or a compliment. "Congratulations. I see you've done your homework, Mr. Delito. Or your attorney's done it."

"Same thing. He's got my back." His words lingered, before he added, "Understand where I'm coming from?"

"I sure do," she replied, trying not to laugh at his implied threat. "You sound like a lousy actor in a bad melodrama. There's no blackmail here, and if you're worried about paparazzi, well— they give me hives, too. So, don't bother calling again unless you want to arrange a meet."

She hung up. He could be the answer to all her problems, or he could be a bigger problem. But to find out, he had to commit.

Her cell rang. "Alexis Brown."

"My house. Two o'clock. I never turn down an invitation from a beautiful woman."

SHE RANG THE BELL at two-fifteen, and the door opened immediately. He must have been watching for her from the window.

"Sorry we're late," she said. "The baby

slept longer than usual, and we missed our train by seconds."

He stood back, allowing her room to wheel the infant inside. "You dragged that stroller onto the T?" he asked, his voice filled with amazement.

She inhaled quickly three times and detected no alcohol on his breath—her first item of business. So far, so good. "Sure," she replied to his question. "We either walk or use public transportation. Last time, we walked here. Today is overcast and colder."

"Next time, use a car service."

Was he kidding? "I work for Suffolk County, Mr. Delito, not for rich private clients who break the law and want a get-out-of-jail card."

His eyes narrowed, his mouth tightened. He seemed to be taking her remark personally, and she hadn't meant it that way at all. Did he have a guilty conscience? This was no way to begin their conversation.

She glanced around the entrance foyer and saw elegance everywhere. "You have a beautiful home, Mr. Delito."

"All Kim's doing."

Suddenly, she was concerned about tracking dirt onto the polished parquet floors of the stately house. She started to voice her concerns, but Dan waved her through to the kitchen in the back. A comfortable room, probably remodeled in recent years, it featured contemporary cabinets and materials, including a beautiful granite countertop.

Alexis unzipped the baby's bunting bag and took off her hat, revealing the beginnings of her strawberry-blonde cap of hair.

"He's a cute kid," said Dan. "Maybe he'll play football one day."

"Not quite," she replied, smiling. "*His* name is Michelle, and she will *not* be a cheerleader. Don't even go there!"

He chuckled for a moment, looking comfortable and relaxed, then leaned his hip against the table and crossed his arms. He looked her in the eye. "So, Alexis Brown. Just why are you here?"

Dan Delito watched the woman pull something from her purse. A picture. Showing it to him, she asked, "Do you recognize her?"

He glanced at the image of a pretty woman, auburn curls, high cheekbones. She called herself Sunshine. "A nice girl with a quick wit. Very funny and upbeat. She was always showing up at the hotels and making herself… shall we say…good company."

"Good com-pan-y?" The woman's eyes were as big and round as dinner plates, her complexion alabaster-white, her voice barely audible as she now whispered, "Just give me a minute. Reality is making a house call."

He'd give her as long as she needed to avoid fainting. He heard her take a deep breath. Saw her shoulders straighten. Watched color return to her cheeks.

"Great recovery, Alexis Brown. You can play on my team anytime at all."

Those hazel eyes flashed golden sparks, enhancing her determined expression. "I hope you mean that." She turned to coo at the baby and give her a soft musical rattle before placing the picture on the table.

"This is Sherri," she began, her index finger on the photo. "The baby is my niece, Sherri's daughter. Sherri was my sister."

Studying the photograph again, he said, "I'm very sorry for your loss, Ms. Brown." He tilted his head toward the baby. "And hers." He allowed silence to grow between them, and in a very soft voice, said, "And what does all this have to do with me?"

Without a word, she rummaged in her purse again, removed an envelope and handed him a newspaper clipping. "I'll give you a minute to read this."

He took it, ready to scan the brief article, but

the murder–suicide mentioned in the headline made him take his time. His lawyer had told him about this, but Dan hadn't seen any of the stories himself. "This is tough," he said slowly, "but again, I ask you—what does this have to do with me?" An unwelcome idea was beginning to form, an idea he and Andy had flirted with, but he wasn't going to put words in the woman's mouth or make it easier for her.

"I was in the ambulance," she began. "I was with Sherri to the…the very end. And the last words she whispered to me before she died were, 'Call Dan Delito…he's the dad.'"

His suspicions were confirmed, but the woman was way off base. Hell, he couldn't even remember the last time he'd been with Sunshine—uh, Sherri. Hadn't he been careful that night? Had the damn condom broken? He had no idea. He usually fell asleep quickly afterward.

"You've got a problem on your hands," he said. "But I'm not the answer." *The best defense was always an offense.* He stepped away from the table and leaned over her. "You and what army are going to make me believe that I'm the father?"

Her blank stare made him chuckle. "Did you really think I'd go along with this? I'm sorry about your sister, Ms. Brown. I truly am. But she was a good-time girl. She could have slept with a dozen guys that month for all I know."

Her lips pressed against each other, her nostrils widened and her complexion flushed to a bright red. Alexis Brown looked ready to blow like an overheated pressure cooker. She had chutzpah, all right, to be angry because he didn't agree with her script.

"She named only one man in that ambulance, Mr. Delito, and that was you."

"Quarterbacks—"

She held up a hand to prevent his reply. "She should have approached you while she was pregnant…."

"But she didn't, because it's not mine."

"I know it's a shock, and I'm sorry about that."

"No, you're not. You're not sorry at all, and I'm not having this conversation without my own lawyer."

She shrugged. "Call anyone you want. I've got nothing to hide. A DNA test will reveal the truth anyway."

She had a point, but he wanted backup. He punched the autodial on his cell. "Andy—I need you here at the house—ASAP. Yep. You got it. Smart man." He disconnected and gestured widely. "Ten minutes. Take off your coat. Make yourself comfortable."

"That was quick service," she said, nodding toward his cell. "The retainer alone must be a fortune."

There was an edgy quality to her tone, and he didn't reply. He'd remember the connotation, however. Money. He wasn't surprised. Most people thought life was all about money. He'd learned differently.

She placed her jacket on a chair and began fussing over the infant, peering at Dan as she worked. "Sherri circled your name in every news clipping she saved. Every time it appeared. Why do you suppose she'd do that?"

A dozen reasons, but he wasn't going there. Professional athletes were easy targets. He quickly thought of three players in the league who'd made headlines last year—not the kind of headlines they'd wanted. All involving women.

"Want a soft drink?" He opened the fridge and pulled out a can of soda for her, poured a vitamin-laced sports drink for himself.

"Oh, sweetheart, you're kicking and talking! You like your freedom, don't you?"

Amazing how her voice changed when she spoke to the infant. The edginess had disappeared. The tenderness and love she showered on that baby…the expression on the woman's face… God, she was beautiful. Her laugh warmed the room. Warmed him. She was still laughing when she requested a plastic bag for the diaper.

"Sure." He started rummaging through the walk-in pantry. He had no idea where his housekeeper kept bags. Relieved to hear the doorbell, he waved Alexis to the shelves. "Your guess is as good as mine. If you can find them, help yourself."

She pointed at two drawers near the sink. "Mind if I try those?"

"Mi casa es su casa," he murmured, heading toward the front of the house.

"Bingo!"

She must have found her quarry. He heard her chatting to the baby while he let Andy inside and quickly briefed him. They entered the kitchen together.

"What the he—?" Andrew Romano, respected new partner in a prestigious Boston law firm, stopped in his tracks, his eyes on Alexis, his complexion now paler than snow. "A doppelgänger," he whispered. "She looks… looks… No wonder she's giving you the shakes."

"I got over that quickly, Andrew. She's not Kim. My wife would never have concocted a scheme like this woman has."

ALEXIS WHIPPED OUT HER business cards and offered one to Dan's friend. He took it. "A scheme, gentlemen? I think not. My professional reputation is on the line." *The best defense was always an offense.*

She extended her hand to Romano. "Alexis Brown, D.A.'s office, although I'm here on personal business. I'm sure Mr. Delito has filled you in." She allowed a question to remain in her voice.

"I'd like to hear it from you," replied the lawyer.

She summarized the situation. "And of course, the point is moot without a DNA test. Which is why I'm here."

"Your reasons wouldn't include cold cash, would they?" asked Dan. "As in extortion? Or on behalf of the tabloids? The gossip rags? I understand they pay a fortune for stories."

His sarcasm hit her like a blow to the gut, and she almost staggered backward. "On my sister's life," she said with quiet dignity, "I haven't shared this information with anyone. Not even with Michelle's social worker."

She ignored Delito and addressed the other attorney. "I suggest we arrange the DNA test privately without a court order." Her eyes rested on the now-sleeping baby. "Michelle and I...well, we don't need another news article.

We don't want publicity any more than your client does."

Romano nodded, but Dan wouldn't stay ignored. "Damn right, we're doing it privately." He glanced at the baby. "She's a cute kid, but I'm not taking her on unless she's one hundred percent mine."

"That's absolutely fair, Mr. Delito. My interest is in child support from the *real* father. So if the test turns out not to be a match, then you'll never see me or the baby again."

"I'll arrange for the team doc and a lab tech to come to Dan's house," said Romano. "You'll hear from me by tomorrow afternoon. We'll take a swab from the baby, of course, but we'll also want a sample from you, Ms. Brown, to verify your relationship to Michelle. Nothing personal, but celebrities are easy targets."

"No problem. I'm her auntie." She glanced toward the window. "It looks like rain. I've got to leave."

"Andy will give you a ride home," said Dan quickly, with a meaningful glance at his friend.

She rattled off her address. "Don't play games with me. If you want to know where I live, just ask. I said I have nothing to hide, and I meant it." She buttoned her coat, zipped Michelle's bunting bag and tucked the blanket around her. "Good evening, gentlemen. We're done here." She headed for the door.

"I insist on giving you a lift," said Romano. "My car's right outside."

"Thanks. But I'm used to public transportation."

"Don't be stubborn," said Dan. "Think of the baby. It's cold now." He turned to his friend. "See what I mean? She's not like Kim at all."

CHAPTER THREE

WAS HE OR WASN'T HE a dad? The DNA swab had been taken on Thursday, and on the field for a Friday practice, Dan's concentration was shot. A bad thing with a game in Philly on Sunday. The Philadelphia Eagles would be ready for them—ready and eager to take them down. But his thoughts kept swirling. He threw the ball like a robot and monitored the field with only a tiny portion of his brain, as though he were watching himself play from afar.

Besides the baby question…there was Alexis Brown. Stubborn, intelligent, bold. And beautiful. Like a chess player, she'd figured out all his moves in advance, covering her shapely ass, anticipating his objections. Not even the presence of his lawyer had shaken her. And in the end, she'd gotten her wish. He'd been suckered into a paternity test.

"Hey, Delito!"

Dan spun around to see Sean Callan, his personal coach, trotting up to him.

"Where's your head right now?"

"Sorry, Coach. I'm with you."

"The hell you are." Callan nodded toward the team. "They're starting to worry about you. Were you drinking last night?"

Startled, Dan stepped back. The guys knew he kept sober on the weekends. "Not a friggin' drop. And I know the playbook cold." Fifty running plays, two hundred passing plays. All choreographed and in his head. Usually. But today…

"Then prove it. Philly wants our blood. If you can't cut it, Rick won't let you start, despite that magic arm of yours. And what am I going to tell him?" he asked, referring to the team's head coach.

"You won't need to tell him anything." Dan jogged to his receiving line. "Pass patterns, guys." Then he called to Sean. "Where's the blindfold?"

The men started to grin. This was the Dan they loved. The Dan they wanted. He knew it, and he wanted it, too. He wanted the respect, the love, the wins. Now they'd have tough fun with exact pass patterns. The players always said that with so much practice, they could run pass patterns in their sleep. A blindfold was the next best thing.

Suddenly, the entire offensive coaching staff was there. Offensive coordinator, and the offensive line coach with head coach, Rick Thompson, watching everyone. Seemed like the whole organization was interested in the skills of Dan Delito.

Dan glanced at Al Tucker. "Five-step-right. Be there." They formed a line of scrimmage at the thirty-yard hash mark. Dan put on the blindfold, called the play, ran his steps and threw the ball. He pulled the eye cover off quickly, in time to see the ball fly right at Tucker's chest. The receiver made a perfect catch and ran with it to the end zone. Fun with no opponents.

Cheers went up, good sounds, solid sounds. Confident sounds.

"What are you all standing around for?" he called. "The coaches are waiting."

Either he was or he wasn't a daddy, and he'd find out on Monday, after the Philly game. Right now, however, he had a job to do.

THE SPECIAL DELIVERY LETTER arrived at Alexis's house at 9:00 a.m. Monday morning. Dan's phone call came at 9:10.

"When can you get over here? We need to talk."

Her hand trembled, holding the letter. She was still staring at it, and had been for the entire ten minutes. "Maybe tomorrow," she blurted. "I need time to get my mind around this."

"Ms. Brown—you've had three months to 'get your mind around it.' I'm the one still reeling. For crying out loud—this news changes my whole life!"

"In a good way or a bad way?" she asked, wishing she could see his expression.

"Hmm…I guess that remains to be seen. Is she a good kid?"

"I think I'll save the congratulations," she muttered.

"Say again? I couldn't hear you."

"Never mind. It's just that theory is different from reality," she said. "The results are real, and I need time to adjust, also. I'll call you tomorrow." And she hung up.

Not her most professional moment, but she'd had no idea the truth would slam her with such force. Make her insecurities shoot skyward. The baby…the baby! What if he simply took her away? She'd been counting on a shared arrangement. Split custody, with Dan providing the funds for child care while she provided the baby with the real home. She'd agree to some weekend arrangement or midweek arrangement for him—whatever worked with his schedule.

But now he was the proven *father*. Suddenly,

the word took on incredible power. How powerful was an aunt? Would Alexis now need her own lawyer to represent her interests? To ensure her presence in Michelle's life?

The phone rang again, and she answered it, feeling as tense as when waiting for a jury verdict.

"Don't hang up."

She tapped her fingers on the table. *Be nice. Be friendly. You need his cooperation.* "Okay. I'm still with you."

"I need your cooperation, Ms. Brown," he began, strangely echoing her own thought. "In fact, we need a little teamwork here."

"In all due respect, Mr. Delito, I think I've already done my part. I've just given you the— the most wonderful gift in the world." Her throat tightened on swallowed sobs. "What more can you possibly want?"

He didn't hesitate. "Your silence—until the organization and I figure out how to release the news without harm done to anyone."

"What organization? Harm? To whom?"

"You're a smart woman, so I'll let you figure that out," he said, his voice patient, calm. "Three, two, one—" he counted.

"Football."

"Knew you'd make the connection."

But of course. The New England Patriots.

The NFL. Little by little, she was beginning to acknowledge that she was dealing with another world right now, a thousand miles out of her league. However, she wasn't out of the game.

"Mr. Delito, I'm sure you understand I care only about Michelle's well-being. A baby is not nurtured by a committee or an 'organization.' She's nurtured by people who love her. You're a big boy. You can handle the rest of it. She is safe and sound with me."

Her career was safe. Her office already knew about Alexis being Michelle's custodian. No problems there.

"Safe and sound? I hope so. For the baby's sake, keep your mouth shut or you'll have photographers at your door before lunchtime."

Silence pounded her ears while his words sank in. She would never, ever call the newspapers, but he was absolutely correct. They'd find her. In Boston, Dan Delito carried the same fame as a Hollywood movie star. In fact, he was sure to be famous on the West Coast, too.

"Oh-h-h…"

"Now do you get it?" he asked quietly.

She sighed. "I get it."

"Ms. Brown," he began again. "Alexis— listen hard. I know you're a smart lawyer who deals with a lot of people with complicated problems. But you've got no experience with aggressive paparazzi. I went through this when my wife died. Headlines everywhere. They were sympathetic, but I was under a microscope anyway. And the situation we have now is, shall we say, nastier. It has salacious overtones, perfect for gossip and melodrama. Frankly, it doesn't get juicier than murder and suicide."

Nice speech, but he was wrong about some things. "Have you forgotten the clipping I showed you at your house, Mr. Delito? My name was in it, too."

"Call me Dan. At this point, we're a team."

Not really, but she said, "Okay, Dan. Unfortunately, I've also been in the papers regarding cases I've handled. And I agree with you. I didn't like it, but it goes with the territory. So, I won't say a word— Oh, dammit! I just remembered— Roz, the social worker, is coming today."

"Cancel the visit," he responded. "And do it now. Then call me back. I need to know about social workers, about doctors. I need to know everything that's happened since the baby's birth." This time, he was the one who disconnected.

Alexis still hadn't told Roz about her search for Dan Delito, the possible father who was now the confirmed father. Speculation helped no one. But now, even in her overwrought state, she knew his identity had larger implications. If she revealed Dan Delito's involvement, could her new friend keep it confidential? Not that Roz would intentionally gossip, but it would go into her report, into a computer. Once others in her office knew, all of Boston would know—and then all of America.

Was that fair to Dan? To Michelle? Or even to her? Her stomach flip-flopped. She, herself, might be the target of gossip all over her office. Suddenly, her strong safety net seemed frayed, the mesh ripped with holes. Her request for family leave, which was almost over, might be looked on with suspicion. Quarterback Dan Delito was a wealthy man. He could have afforded a slew of child-care providers. And now the story would hit the papers. Not good. Dan was right. It was better to control the news than be victimized by a leak.

Okay. Her brain was working again. One step at a time. She picked up the phone.

"Roz, hi. It's Alexis. I think I'm coming down with a nasty cold. Could we postpone our visit until later this week? So sorry for the last-minute notice."

She listened to advice about face masks and chicken soup, and felt guilty about her white lie. Roz had become as close a friend as Alexis had ever had. She hoped the woman would later agree that the circumstances had been extraordinary. Extraordinary enough to warrant a little deception.

DAN KNEW ONLY ENOUGH about babies to realize they were a lot of trouble. A lot of work. But that would come later. Now, he should call his lawyer, his agent, his coach, the head coach, the club's owner—all of his businesspeople—and, of course, his family. *Mama mia,* his mother! His dad. But as he waited for Alexis to call him back, he sat in his kitchen, immobile, thinking only about the baby…and the baby's aunt.

The woman haunted him every time he had a minute to relax. And then he'd think about Kim. The two women were physically similar only at first glance. Their true resemblance was revealed when Alexis showed her love for that baby. When she nuzzled the infant, her features softened, and her sweetness overflowed. In those special moments, his heart almost stopped and Kim's name rose to his tongue. So far, he'd been able to clamp his jaw shut. But he'd never forgotten how Kim had yearned to be a mom.

He had no doubt that the lawyer loved her niece, so he wouldn't shut her out. He'd allow her to visit him and the baby from time to time—

after he figured out how to become a little family with Michelle. A family. Kim should have been part of this family. She should have had the chance. A child would have been the most fantastic touchdown in their personal lives.

Damn, he needed a drink.

He reached into the fridge for a brewski, then glanced at his watch and groaned. Too early— even he knew that. He slammed the refrigerator door, felt beads of sweat pop out on his skin. He wanted that beer. Time to change focus.

The woman hadn't phoned him back yet. Ten minutes was enough time for a quick call to the social worker. He glanced at Alexis's business card and punched in her number again. Next step was to enter it into his cell's autodial.

"Alexis Brown."

"What's wrong?" Her voice sounded funny. Nasal. As if she'd been crying.

"Nothing. What do you want?"

"You were supposed to call me back. How did you make out with the social worker?"

"She believed me, but I hate lying."

At least Alexis wasn't crying anymore. "I'm coming over to your place. Let me in when I buzz."

"Have you called…whoever it is you need to call?"

"No. No one." He probably should, but he was going with his gut right now, following his instincts as he did a lot in the game. Independent judgment trumped prearranged plans more often than people would imagine.

But now all he said was, "We need to—to talk. To figure things out first." Like figure out if he was happy about being a father or not.

"I guess we can't meet at the Frog Pond or in the Gardens…?" Her voice was wishful and came slowly, as though she were thinking out loud.

"Sorry, not if we want privacy. Notice that I'm willing to meet on your turf." It had taken time, but he'd become used to arranging his life partly for the public and partly for himself. With the DNA test behind him, he could afford to be generous and go to Alexis's apartment.

"Of course," she said. "No Frog Pond. You're too well-known, and we definitely do want privacy. I'll make some coffee or something."

"Don't bother, Alexis. It's not exactly a social visit."

He heard her gasp and immediately knew he'd said the wrong thing.

"Do you consider meeting your daughter a business transaction, Mr. Delito?"

"Of course not. And I said to call me Dan. Let's back up a step. Maybe we do need a little time to digest everything, and I sure need time in the hot tub. How about one o'clock? I'll come over then."

She readily agreed, and he hung up. It wasn't a very auspicious beginning, though. She sounded as if she'd been reprieved from a hanging.

HE WAS BIGGER THAN SHE remembered him, full of energy, full of power, and way too handsome with a lock of dark hair hanging over his forehead. If she'd met him at a party, she would have danced with him—as long as he wasn't drinking.

"No limp today," she said. "Hot tub must have worked. Have a seat." Chatter, chatter, nervous chatter.

"Nice place you've got," he said, scanning the apartment. "Spacious. They did a good job with the conversion. And they saved the brickwork."

Funny how he immediately identified her favorite part of the house. The brick made the open space feel warm and cozy.

"It was the top selling point when I decided to buy the place," she said.

"So, you own? Not rent?"

She nodded. "With a heavy mortgage, but it's mine."

"Ergo, no car."

She waved his words away. "On the trains I'm

only two stops away from the Common and the Gardens and just as close to my office. Why would I bother with a car?"

"To cart the baby around more easily?"

"Don't underestimate the power of a devoted aunt," she replied, meeting his gaze. Then she wished she hadn't.

His eyes narrowed, his brow furrowed. His big hands now rested on his hips. A power stance.

Maybe she should have called Roz. She hated being in a weak position. So she squared her shoulders and stood taller.

"Speaking of…" he said. "Where's the baby?"

"'The baby' has a name. Why don't you try using it?"

He studied her before replying. "And why are you so snippy with me? The Brown part of her name is going to change. That's for sure."

Well, that was the easiest thing to accept. Alexis glanced at the man with the determined expression. Seemed he'd done a lot of thinking in the last few hours, and she tried bracing herself for a slew of other changes that were sure to come. She'd handle them all and make Dan happy, as long as her life with Michelle remained intact.

She led him into her bedroom, where she'd converted one corner into a nursery. Quietly, they approached the crib. Michelle lay on her back, eyes closed, sound asleep. Alexis watched her little chest move up and down and relaxed. Sometimes, at night, she'd put her fingers under the baby's nose just to make sure she was breathing. She often wondered if every new mother did the same.

She glanced at Dan, but he was simply staring at his daughter. His lids didn't blink. He stood frozen, not moving a muscle, except a tiny one in his jaw. Shock. Awe. Fear. Lost in his own world and overwhelmed. Joy rose inside her, filling her to the very brim. She stepped away, leaving him alone by the crib.

"Where are you going?" A hoarse whisper— possibly tinged with panic?

"I'm right here," she affirmed, her heart dancing for the first time since she'd made the decision to contact him. Dan was the father, but he was more frightened by a ten-pound baby than by the gladiators on the gridiron. A perfect situation, as far as Alexis was concerned. She'd provide the home and child care, while he supplied the check.

DAN STARED AT THE MOST beautiful baby in the world. His daughter. His child. And wanted to run away. A million decisions awaited him. A million arrangements…and lots of stuff to buy. He had a game against the Cowboys this weekend. It wasn't even midseason yet; there was a long way to go, and he couldn't screw up. Should he hire a baby nurse and take the kid out of town with him? Should he ask his mother? But she and his dad had a business to run. Should he hire a live-in housekeeper? Maybe two of them? Man, a tiny baby needed a lot of care.

He faced Alexis. "She's so little," he whispered.

"Absolutely, but time will cure that." Her eyes gleamed with amusement.

The lawyer actually had a sense of humor. He tilted his head toward the door and started to leave the room. "Let her sleep."

Alexis nodded her agreement and smiled at him again. Whew. She had a killer smile. A happy smile. Finally, a genuine smile that brightened her face. Okay. He was starting to read her body language, a skill he was…supposedly…good at.

In the kitchen once again, he inhaled the aroma of coffee. "You did make a pot after all."

"Want some?"

"Sure." He watched her pour. Confident now. No shaky hands or voice.

When they were both seated, he said, "First

things first. I've got a game in Dallas this weekend."

She held up her palm. "No problem, Dan. The baby's living with me anyway. In fact, to be perfectly honest…"

He hated that phrase. It was usually followed by something that wasn't honest at all.

"…I don't quite know what my sister's intention was when she revealed your name to me at the end. But I don't imagine it was for you to be involved with Michelle's day-to-day care."

The heart of the matter. A setup. She was setting him up for a one-two punch.

"Oh?" He kept his voice neutral. Let her keep talking before he reacted.

"Think about it," Alexis continued. "She never told you about the baby. She knew what your schedule was like—" she blinked hard and turned away for a moment "—probably better than you did. And—and I know she planned to raise the baby herself…with my help." She leaned toward him. "I asked, but she never told me your name until the end. Until she probably felt she had no other choice."

Her eyes were too shiny. *Please don't cry, lady.* Whenever Alexis brought up her sister, a waterfall threatened. But now she was chatting again.

"So, knowing your hectic lifestyle and her

plans, I don't think she had in mind for you to actually be in charge of Michelle…at least, not now."

Her last words were rushed, as though she were trying to appease him. Dan thought of his own dad. Of his family. His parents lived and breathed for their kids, for their six grandkids. They'd worked hard building their grocery and deli business so their children could have the advantages they hadn't. And Alexis Brown was trying to tell the son of Nicky Delito to abandon his daughter?

It wasn't going to happen. But he wasn't ready to shut down the conversation.

"Not be in charge of my daughter, Alexis?" he asked quietly. "Then why am I here? Are we back to extortion?"

"Good grief, no! I don't need *that* kind of money. I've known how to stretch a dollar since I was a kid. With careful use of my funds, and a tiny bit of help for day care, I can support my niece just fine."

She spoke the truth and he relaxed slightly—until another truth popped up, an incredible truth that made his blood pressure rise, that scared the wits out of him. That made him use real effort to keep his voice at a reasonable pitch.

"So, the only reason—the single reason—honorable attorney Alexis Brown contacted me at all was because of a few dollars for child care?"

HIS ATTACK KNOCKED THE breath from Alexis's body. Surely he didn't want to be deeply involved in Michelle's care? He didn't make sense. He was a single man. He traveled constantly. Hell, a couple of weeks ago, he hadn't even known he *had* a daughter. Was he serious?

She willed herself to inhale again and wrestled control of her mind. If two years in the D.A.'s office had taught her nothing else, they had taught her how to stay focused on a goal in the face of determined opposition. And she had to stay focused. Dan was her last hope. If she alienated him, she would likely have to put Michelle in foster care. And that was no place for the child Sherri had entrusted to Alexis's care.

Dan was staring at her. She had to respond to his accusation. *The best defense is an offense*, she thought for the second time in a week.

"Michelle is three months old," she said. "How much quicker would you have acted if your sister had been killed, given birth and left you with a newborn infant, not to mention dealing with cops and social workers? How much faster could you have set up a nursery, gotten a leave from work and learned how to care for a newborn? Did you think it all happened by osmosis?"

So what if he'd guessed the true reason—at least, the immediate reason—for her daddy search? She'd been living one day at a time for awhile and doing the best she could.

He put up his hands. "Whoa. Okay, okay. Points taken," he said quietly, "but you haven't answered the question."

"And I'm not going to."

Standoff. Hazel eyes challenged brown as they stared at each other in silence. Adrenaline shot through Alexis's body, raising her awareness of details—the creases in the corners of his eyes, the slight cleft in his chin, the arch in his eyebrow. Like taking a series of snapshots, she memorized the parts of his face. His size didn't intimidate her, nor did his righteous indignation. In fact, she felt no fear at all.

"Stubborn woman," he muttered.

"Suspicious man," she replied.

They both heard Michelle's cries at the same time and, together, headed toward the bedroom. The baby was kicking and waving at the colorful mobile hanging overhead, but when she saw Alexis, she doubled her speed and cried harder.

"Oh, sweet pea," Alexis crooned, scooping her up. "You're all wet and—" she sniffed the diaper "—dirty, too. Come on, my sweet and stinky petunia. We'll make you nice and clean." The baby calmed down to a hiccup or two, as she usually did when Alexis held her.

Alexis stepped in front of the big man and went to the changing table, where all the appropriate equipment and toiletries were within easy reach.

Dan hadn't moved.

Alexis glanced behind her. "Dirty diapers are part of the deal."

"Hmm…I—I don't want to interfere."

If only.

Michelle turned her head toward his voice. "She's looking for you," said Alexis, her gaze darting toward him again. "If you can't handle this, she'll wind up with a painful diaper rash."

His suntanned complexion paled. "Painful?" he asked as he strode toward the baby.

Maybe he was rethinking any plans he might be formulating about becoming a full-time dad. *Good.*

Michelle stared at him as Alexis worked. No gurgling. No crying. Just staring.

"Talk to her," said Alexis. "She usually vocalizes a bit when she wakes up."

"What should I say?"

She didn't know whether to laugh or cry. She was comforted, however, because he knew so little. He wouldn't want to take over Michelle's care when the scope of the responsibility hit him.

Which was just as it should be. Dan hadn't been in Sherri's plan at all. Her sister had never mentioned him. Sherri had, however, counted on Alexis—Auntie Alexis—to be part of Michelle's life. All the planning they'd done, the shopping, the child-care books they'd read together… Alexis and Sherri had gotten closer during the pregnancy. Sherri had been taking responsibility and making plans to return to school. Alexis had been proud of her for that.

It wasn't until the end, in that ambulance, that Sherri had finally shared the truth. Was it because Alexis would be alone and need help? That was the only reason Alexis could imagine. But now, by approaching Dan, she might have started something she'd be sorry for. His "help" could turn into an arrangement Sherri wouldn't have wanted, either.

She needed to gain Dan's trust, tear down his defenses.

"Tell her how smart and beautiful she is," Alexis suggested. "Tell her how the sun is shining in her window. Anything at all. Just talk."

He followed her first idea, then went off on his own. "Daddy will hire two nurses. No diaper rash for you, baby girl. And after the season, we'll go to Florida and have a vacation on the boat, and go to Disney. All little kids love Disney, and you will, too. And we'll take your cousins."

The baby remained quiet, watching him, and he beamed at Alexis. "How am I doing?"

"Great," she muttered. "Just great." She envisioned wild parties with his teammates on his yacht. She moved her head slightly to look at him. "If you have parties on that boat, drinking is out, you know. Trust me, when you're caring for an infant, everything in your life changes. Everything."

"Then I guess it will change," Dan asserted.

Her stomach knotted and dots of perspiration covered her. Fear had invaded, and she needed a minute by herself. "I'm going to warm her bottle."

"Wait. You can't leave me alone with her."

He was right. She couldn't risk it, not when panic laced his voice. Alexis lifted Michelle and glanced at Dan. "Come on, Daddy," she began, with an emphasis on the title. "You'll hold her on the couch first." She sensed his panic subsiding. "I thought you had a slew of nephews and nieces."

"I do. But I didn't change their diapers, or feed them when they ate mush, for that matter." His voice trailed off as if he was back in time, remembering. "I played with them. You know—on the floor. In the backyard. On the street. We'd throw a ball, they'd climb all over me and we'd have a great time. In fact, we still do."

"Oh, I'm sure you do. And I'm also sure you waited until they were out of diapers before you got involved with them," she said. "You don't have that option now, if you're serious."

"I'm as serious as a Hail Mary pass," he said, sitting down on the sofa. He lifted his arms for Michelle when Alexis approached. "You can count on it."

She'd be a fool not to and wanted to weep. "You'll be fine here. She can't get hurt. I'll bring the bottle right away."

Finally, she escaped to the kitchen. Dan Delito claiming Michelle on a full-time basis wasn't what she'd envisioned at all. He was Boston's golden boy, a young Turk so busy with a demanding career…always traveling or practicing…with so much money and prestige, so much power….

She slapped her forehead as all the pieces came together. Sherri must have worried about the same thing—that Dan Delito had the clout to simply take the baby from her, a good-time girl working at low-wage jobs. How could Alexis have been so naive as to not realize that right away?

She was busy for less than a minute when she heard, "Wow! What a smile. Come here, Alexis. Look at her. She's beautiful. Holy cow! I think she's flirting with me. How can that be?"

"I have no idea." And she didn't. She'd never practiced those feminine wiles herself, didn't trust them, didn't use them. She couldn't remember ever playing little girl games with her father. Not that her avoidance had helped.

"Michelle's simply gorgeous," said Alexis. "She's probably just feeling good, and you're a new distraction."

"I agree about the gorgeous part. Abso-pos-a-tutely."

Alexis brought the bottle over and saw a grinning Michelle looking straight up at her dad. The man was a goner. Right over the moon.

But nothing brought more excitement than the promise of the bottle. The baby spotted it, kicked and waved at it. Alexis looked at Dan, then at the formula. Him? Or herself? *Cooperate. Be friendly. Remember the short-term pain and long-term gain philosophy.* With a huge sigh, she handed the milk to Dan and once again disappeared into the kitchen, leaving him alone with his daughter.

One thing she knew for sure: a parent had more clout than an aunt in court. She could fight him, but what chance did she have of winning? Less than none. She needed Dan to *want* to share the baby. Of course, she now understood the chance of that happening was less than none, as well.

CHAPTER FOUR

"A BABY! WHAT ARE YOU talking about?"

In his parents' large country kitchen, Dan's mother clutched his arm, her trembling voice revealing the anxiety reflected on her face. His normally upbeat mom wasn't acting too upbeat today. In fact, she hadn't been very happy in a long time, at least not with him. He'd disappointed her, disappointed his dad and a pang of guilt pierced him, made him want to reach for some single malt. He clenched his hands into fists and felt his biceps and triceps tighten up. Then he relaxed his muscles. A good quick stress reliever.

On the evening after his visit to Alexis and Michelle, he'd invited himself for dinner at his parents' house. Andy Romano had already started on the legal paperwork for court. Alexis had promised to call the social worker and arrange a meeting. All Dan had to do was tell his folks the news. Obviously, he wasn't doing too good a job of it.

"Ma, why don't you sit down? It's good news, at least most of it is. I'm talking about my three-month-old daughter."

"Three months! And you never told us?"

He appealed to his dad. "She's going to have a stroke. Make her sit down."

"She's not the only one. What the hell are you talking about, Danny? What baby? Where's the mother? Did you get married in secret?"

Married? Was his dad nuts? Dan had no plans in that direction.

"Of course I'm not married. But things happen sometimes…you know…like after a game." He hoped they'd get the picture without a detailed drawing.

"Oh my God! Nicky, did you hear him?" His mom grabbed his dad's hand. "'After a game,' he says. It's got to be one of those girls, one of those run-around girls who always follow the team. Out for a good time. Out for their money."

His mom could barely look at him. "How could you, Danny, how could you?" Her words ended on a wail, lingering in the air. "Especially after a wonderful girl like Kim…"

"This has nothing to do with Kim," he protested. Except, of course, it had everything to do with her. The groupies allowed him to forget for a while.

"So, what's it going to cost you in support?" his practical dad interrupted. "I assume you've gotten proof?"

"Oh, Michelle's mine, all right," said Dan, his spirits lifting despite his folks' reaction to the news. "She's the cutest, most perfect little baby, no bigger than a football. Yesterday, I gave her a bottle. Wait till you see her…."

Nick held his hand up like a cop. "Stop. I'll tell you right now that's not happening until I know everything."

Dan filled them in, spinning out the story, and watched their reactions. His mom was an easy read. Tears and horror came at Sherri's murder, then awe at the delivery in the ambulance, pity for a motherless baby, sympathy for Alexis at first, then a question at Alexis's waiting three months. By the end of his recital, Rita was on the couch, frozen in her seat, murmuring, "Oh my, oh my…" licking her lips and shaking her head.

"How can you trust this…this Alexis Brown?" asked Nicky. "She probably wants fifty percent of everything you've got."

"Who said anything about trust?" replied Dan. "I'm the father. Alexis has no claim to the baby, other than some visiting now and then. Andy will figure that out."

"I bet she can't wait to dump the kid on you," said his dad.

Maybe if he were hearing the story for the first time, Dan would react exactly as his father had. But now, he wanted to be fair. Alexis had done a great job with Michelle. At some point, Rita and Nicky would probably meet Alexis, and Dan preferred to avoid an awkward encounter.

"That's not true. Alexis can wait, all right." He closed his eyes, picturing the lawyer's expressive face as she played with the baby. "That's not the problem, Dad. She loves Michelle…actually too much. I saw them together. According to Alexis, she's the real mom now."

Nicky's whistle was long and low. "The real mom? Danny-boy, you've got yourself a problem."

Dan chuckled wryly. "Oh, I've got lots of problems, but Alexis Brown isn't one of them. She's an attorney. She knows the score. I'll only see her from time to time in the future, when she visits Michelle."

He'd say goodbye to those sparkly green eyes and lovely curves, the cute bottom that made his hand itch, and the great legs—not to mention the sharp mind. He'd almost enjoyed their sparring.

Rita stared at him, her complexion back to healthy. "You don't sound too happy about that, Dan. And besides, maybe you should be friendly toward her. You might need her help with the baby."

"I've already had her help, and now I simply owe her a debt of thanks. She's taken excellent care of my daughter." Might as well emphasize his fatherhood and get his folks used to it.

"When can we meet this paragon of a woman?" asked Nicky. "We need to know who we're dealing with."

Surprised at his dad's question, Dan said, "You don't need to meet her at all. In a week, it won't matter. Michelle will be with me full-time. We'll transfer her to my house next week, after I get back from Baltimore." With hope in his heart, he added, "And grandparents are always welcome."

"I'M SO SORRY IT turned out this way, Alexis, but you did the right thing."

Alexis accepted the hugs and sympathy from Roz three weeks after Dan had come to her place. Her fears had been confirmed. Dan was in; Alexis was out—as of today—per expedited orders of the probate court. By some miracle, Roz wasn't as angry with her for withholding the information about Dan Delito as she would have thought.

"Under ordinary circumstances, I'd have been furious," the social worker said, "but I can understand your reluctance to spread rumors if Dan Delito had turned out *not* to be the dad. In fact, we might have created bad publicity for the department."

"It's the celebrity thing."

Roz shrugged. "Blame the public."

Tears rolled down Alexis's cheeks once more. "I blame myself. Why did I not foresee something like this? At the very worst, I thought shared custody…. What should I have, could I have done differently to keep Michelle with me?"

"Not a single thing." Roz paused. "Look at me, Alexis. Hear me out. And believe me."

Alexis stared at her friend.

"You did everything right, and life just sucks sometimes. Despite your pain, you've given your niece a gift that no one else in this entire world could have given her. The gift of a real daddy and a big family. You know we've checked him out, regardless of his great public image, and he's the real McCoy. A clean background. Michelle's getting herself a good daddy."

As long as he didn't drink to excess. As long as her first meeting with him was an aberration.

"And my parents are out of the visitation picture entirely. Right?"

"Absolutely." Roz stared at her. "Want to talk about them?"

"I have nothing to say. They're a closed chapter."

Roz squeezed her arm. "Okay."

They both tiptoed to the crib and peeped at the baby for a full minute. Alexis's breathing became labored as she fought tears again. In one hour, her life and Michelle's would change. Dan would arrive to take the baby, and Alexis would remain in an empty apartment. Tomorrow, and every night thereafter, only silence would be her companion in the condo. Closing her eyes, she already sensed the loneliness.

She heaved a deep breath and straightened her spine. *Suck it up, kiddo. No pity parties.* Michelle will have every advantage you and Sherri didn't—a loving daddy, a beautiful home, lots of toys and plenty of young cousins.

"I'm petitioning the probate court for visiting rights," she said to Roz when they returned to the living room. "I'd be a fool to trust Dan Delito's promises. All he's thinking about is his new daughter. He won't care about me at all after he gets Michelle."

"You may be right," replied Roz quietly, "but

don't forget, you got what you wanted, too." She raised a finger as she made her points. "You're back at work right on schedule this Monday, your day-care problem is solved and your money worries are over."

Alexis sighed. "I should have been more careful with my wishes." Or she should have become a defense attorney with rich clients and a big bank account.

When the buzzer rang from the lobby, nausea rose, threatening to overpower her. With a trembling hand, she pushed the release button to let Dan inside and waited for him on the threshold of her condo.

"I'm going downstairs with you." The sentence tumbled out of her mouth as soon as she saw him. She didn't know she would say those words, hadn't planned on saying them, but they rolled off her tongue as a done deal. She didn't ask, she stated.

His eyes narrowed, his tentative smile disappeared entirely. "May I come in?"

"Of course." *Not.* But she stepped aside and watched his expression change to one of delight when he spotted the baby in Roz's arms. He made a beeline to Michelle and peered down at his daughter.

"Hello, sweet petunia."

My sweet petunia.

But the baby reacted with her usual excitement, waving her arms, moving her legs at the man. And with one feathery motion, Dan slipped Michelle from Roz's arms into his own. So quick. So definite. So possessive. Then he looked at Alexis.

"Coming to the car is not a good idea." His gaze traveled all over her. "You're on the verge of a meltdown already, and you'd only prolong the goodbye." He glanced at the social worker. "Don't you agree?"

Roz's arm came around Alexis. Warm, sure, comforting.

But Alexis was beyond comfort. The reality was worse, much worse, than she could have imagined. Her insides trembled as though she were a rag doll with every limb dancing its own cha-cha.

"How will she travel?" Her voice was raspy, her throat hurt. "Did you buy the right toiletries? Who will take care of her tomorrow?"

And that's when she saw compassion in his face, warmth in his dark eyes as he looked at her. "It's all arranged, Alexis," he said quietly. "Don't worry about a thing. My mom, who's raised three children, is coming tomorrow morning. We've got a home game this weekend against Dallas, and the rest of the family will meet Michelle afterward. I'm also calling a nanny agency to provide full-time help."

He walked toward her, raised his free arm and stroked her cheek. "I'm not a monster, Alexis Brown. Call me to arrange a visit."

Then he turned to Roz. "My attorney's downstairs in the car. Are we squared away?"

Roz nodded. "The paperwork's done. The baby's been delivered. She's legally yours now, Mr. Delito. Good luck to you and Michelle. Just one more thing…"

He waited.

"I sincerely hope, for Michelle's sake if not for her aunt's, that you're generous with visiting arrangements for Alexis. A child can't have too many loving relatives, and Auntie Alexis tops the list. She's kept your daughter safe and whole." Her soft voice still managed to exude authority and professionalism, as well as loyalty to her client. Alexis wanted to cheer.

"I'll do what I can. My schedule's hectic, though—Alexis knows that."

He approached Alexis. "I bought her the top-of-the-line car seat that converts to a stroller, her dresser is filled with clothes and there's plenty of formula in the kitchen. She'll be fine." He looked at the baby. "Won't you, Michelle?"

But Michelle had spotted Alexis and begun crying and waving her arms again. Without thinking twice, Alexis scooped her away from the big man. "I'm going downstairs to the car."

His mouth tightened, and he shook his head. "Fine. But it will only be harder on you."

Five minutes later, after tucking Michelle into her new car seat, Alexis stood in front of her building and watched Dan's automobile slowly disappear down the street. It reached the corner, stopped for a red light, then continued until it was a speck in the distance. A moment later, it became invisible.

"I'll stay with you for a while," said Roz. "Come on upstairs."

But Alexis remained frozen to the spot, unsure if her heart continued to beat, but absolutely sure that in heaven, Sherri was crying along with her.

AT MIDNIGHT, DAN FOUND himself lying on the floor in the baby's room, more exhausted than after a field practice. Michelle just wouldn't settle down. He'd fed her, burped her, even changed a full diaper, and still she'd been cranky. Finally, around ten o'clock, she'd fallen asleep in his arms. By that time, however, he'd been afraid to put her in the crib in case she woke up again, as she'd done earlier. So, he'd kept walking and holding her—for two hours.

And all the while, he thought about Kim. He missed her so damn much. He fought the lump in his throat, fought the urge for some alcoholic relief. That urge—that strong urge—always came over him in tandem with his grief. He could see that relationship now. When he thought about Kim, he wanted a drink. He'd have to fight harder.

When twelve o'clock struck, he held his breath, and as gently as he could, placed Michelle in the crib. She continued sleeping. Fatigue overcame his urge for a Scotch, and he dropped to the sleeping bag he'd placed on the floor earlier. His own comfortable bed teased from just down the hall, but he stayed put in case Michelle cried again. His lids closed.

All he needed was a good nanny. Andy Romano's law firm had done the research, and Dan's agent had made the calls, keeping Dan's identity a secret. As he'd told both men earlier, he wanted an experienced nanny, someone with good common sense. Someone who didn't give a hoot about football and fame and could keep her mouth shut. She had to be kind and sweet with his daughter. She had to be someone he could trust when he was on the road.

"And if I find that supernanny," his agent had said, "I might keep her for myself!"

Dan had laughed. "Fat chance. Your wife's all about your kids. No nannies in your house."

He tossed and turned on top of the sleeping bag.

Interviews were set for Monday. Tomorrow, Friday, he had a day of weight training at the stadium; a night's sleep would help but was now unlikely. He'd spend Saturday at home watching videos of the Dallas Cowboys. Sunday was game day, and mental toughness was king. He started visualizing himself on the field, doing what he needed to do, passing the ball off, running or standing in the pocket waiting for his receiver to get open while, at the same time, bracing himself to be taken down. The images started to blur, to fade; his muscles relaxed; his breathing became even….

What? What? He jumped from his bedroll and almost crashed against the crib. The baby was screaming her head off. Dan glanced at the window—still dark outside. Seemed his daughter couldn't tell time yet. He peered into her red face, her mouth open, eyes shut tight, and reached into the crib.

"Okay, baby. Let's figure this out."

It had become one hell of a night, and it wasn't over.

"DAN! IT'S ONLY EIGHT o'clock in the morning, and your eyes are bloodshot. Please don't tell me you've been drinking already?"

Why did his mother always assume the worst? He opened the front door wider and stood aside. "Come on in, Mom." She swooped in, his dad right behind her.

"If my eyes are red, blame your granddaughter. I've been up and down for hours. And now—when's it's finally daytime—she's sleeping."

Rita's chuckle became full-throated laughter. "Oh, my goodness. I guess you are a real daddy after all."

"I can only stay five minutes, Danny-boy," said Nick. "Where is she?" His dad and Joe would work the store alone today. Rita would be missed.

"Follow me, but if you wake her…" His idle threat was treated with amusement. "The kid's got lung power, that's for sure," said Dan. He yawned twice, then stretched his entire body just to get moving.

"How are you going to play on Sunday?" demanded Nicky. "Look at you. You're exhausted."

"It'll be easier when she has a nanny." He covered his mouth as he yawned for a third time.

"Get a couple of hours' sleep now, Danny. I'm here for the day," Rita said.

He nodded. "Right after we peep in on her." Better to be late but ready for his workout than to show up on time and accomplish nothing. Lateness, however, could not become a habit.

They walked up to the third floor, which contained the three bedrooms of the town house, and tiptoed into Michelle's room.

Dan stood back and watched his parents' reservations melt like ice cream on a summer's day, as they viewed their newest grandchild for the first time. Michelle lay on her back in a bunting—no blankets—just the way Alexis had instructed him. It was safer this way.

"She's beautiful, Danny," whispered Rita, her eyes filling and her hands hovering over the infant.

"Don't wake her up!" Dan whispered. "Let's go."

They made it as far as the door before Michelle demonstrated her lung power. Dan closed his eyes and leaned against the wall, the pulse in his temple starting to throb. The first night with his daughter did not bode well for his immediate future. He wondered if Michelle woke up every night or if she'd slept through at Alexis's place.

After his two-hour nap, Dan's cell rang just as he was leaving for the stadium.

"So, how did it go?"

He recognized the woman's voice immediately. Her anxious voice.

"Not to worry, Auntie. She slept like a top." *Liar.*

"Really?" It was almost a squeal. "I'm so relieved. I—I thought…well, I didn't know what to think, so I was up all night. You must have a magic touch."

He could picture her pacing, moving, smiling. "Didn't she sleep through at your place?"

"Sure," said Alexis, "if you consider six hours sleeping through. Usually from about ten at night to four in the morning, and then wham-oh! She screamed for that bottle."

The woman sounded so cheerful about interrupted sleep, while all Dan wanted to do was crash to the floor. Again.

BY SATURDAY MORNING, ALEXIS had polished her condo to a shine. Not a speck of dust lived. Her business suits hung with their matched blouses ready to be worn to the office again, starting Monday. All of Michelle's clothes and toiletries were organized and waiting for her when she visited. Alexis had kept herself busy, busy, busy, wiping tears away as she worked. She missed Michelle—the baby who felt like her daughter. And now, with the weekend still ahead of her, she had nothing more to do.

She glanced out the window. A sunny day beckoned, and she put on her running shoes and a headband. With her cell and a few dollars zipped in her pocket, and a bud in her ear, she cranked her iPod and headed out.

She hadn't lied to Dan about their hometown. Boston was a walking city, a city of parks and running trails, and the historic Freedom Trail, which was a Mecca for tourists. She had pushed Michelle's stroller for miles. Fresh air was good for children, including babies, and exercise was good for her.

Today, she could jog to the Public Gardens, or she could jog down Boylston Street and window-shop along the way. She had lots of lovely choices. So it seemed strange that an hour after leaving her condo, she found herself on the corner of Chestnut Street—Dan Delito's street in the historic Beacon Hill section. She hadn't planned the roundabout route—not consciously—but here she was, slowing down her pace to a walk while her heart rate actually increased. Weird what a case of nerves could do.

She palmed her cell and pushed Dan's number. The man had invited her to call and arrange a visit.

"Hi, Alexis."

"Caller ID?"

"You bet. And you're on it."

Hmm…that actually didn't sound too bad. "I happen to be in the neighborhood, and I was wondering about stopping off for a few minutes." *Please, please, please.*

"Not a good idea right now. Sorry. Tomorrow's the game, and today's my day to relax at home and keep the muscles loose. No weight training, no practices. So it's a good day for Michelle and me to pal around and get to know each other better."

She blinked back tears, now clearly realizing how much she'd counted on the visit. And how little authority she had. "I see. So when do you think—"

"Ahh-ohh."

"Excuse me?"

"Sorry, that was a yawn." A second yawn followed.

"So, how many hours of sleep did you actually get?" asked Alexis.

An empty silence followed her question.

"Dan?"

"Give me a minute. I'm thinking."

Or still sleeping on his feet.

"Here's an idea that might appeal to you," Dan said. "The game's tomorrow, and a sitter won't be coming until Monday. Would you want to stay here tonight and look after Michelle so I can actually sleep? My folks will be over in the morning, so you'd be free then. This time, they're watching a home game on television instead of at the stadium."

Did she want an evening with Michelle? Was the sky blue? "I'll be over at…how about five, so the baby and I can have time to play?"

"You sound like a little kid yourself, Alexis." His deep voice was warm, friendly and amused.

"You've just made me very happy, so if I come across like a kid, so what?"

"Fair warning—don't get used to it. I admit, I'm stuck right now, but next week I won't be. We'll set up a schedule soon."

Suddenly, "warm and friendly" evaporated, but she never went down without a fight.

"A generous schedule, I hope. Remember, Dan, that with me, you're getting a 'value-added' component in a sitter and an aunt. I happen to love your daughter."

AT FIVE O'CLOCK THAT evening, Dan opened the front door and lost his breath. Why did he always forget how pretty Alexis was? That smile could dazzle a man into forgetting who he was and what had been.

"So, where is she?" Alexis reached into her tote bag and held up a small package. "First, though, I need to put this in the fridge, if you don't mind." She headed down the center hall toward the kitchen as though she owned the place.

"What is it?" asked Dan.

"My dinner. A tuna-fish sandwich. It's the only thing I had handy." She peered at him from beneath her lashes. "I'll share if you're hungry."

Oh, his hunger was rising, all right, but not for a sandwich. Those eyes of hers had darkened to a green velvet like rich moss. Her hair was gathered loosely at the nape of her neck. He wanted to pull the elastic away and free the thick mass, he wanted to touch it and run his hands through it. He wanted a lot of things he couldn't have anymore.

"That sandwich wouldn't fill a cavity in my teeth, let alone the one in my stomach. Besides, a sandwich is not a dinner. You'll eat what I eat tonight."

"You don't have to feed me," she said, placing her food in the refrigerator.

He laughed. "I'm Rita and Nicky Delito's son. I grew up in a kitchen, feeding people. Besides, tonight's meal is important because it provides the fuel for tomorrow's game. It's more important than what I eat tomorrow."

She twirled and faced him. "Scientific, huh?"

"Absolutely."

"Where's Michelle?"

"Upstairs."

"By herself?" she squealed.

"Calm down. The house has an intercom system, so I can hear her if she cries. But let's go. You'll feel better when you see her." He hustled them up the stairs to the second floor. Then he led Alexis into his huge game room, where she made a beeline toward the crib.

Michelle was asleep. Dan was content to watch Alexis stare at her niece. *Devour her niece* was more apt. She embraced Michelle visually as though they'd been apart for months, not two days. Her love for that baby was easy to see, and for the first time, Dan's confidence wavered.

He tamped down his uncertainty. He was the father! He and Kim had longed to be parents and Michelle was the child they couldn't have together. The baby belonged with him. Period.

Alexis approached him now. "So, you bought two cribs?"

He nodded. "Of course. There's one upstairs in her bedroom, but I almost live in the game room here," he said with a wide gesture, "when

I'm not training. Pool table, card table, hi-def television, small fridge. Here's where I study videos. So Michelle has to have a comfortable place with me."

She gazed around the huge room, which ran the width of the house. "Wow! From babyhood to teenage-hood, she'll have everything a girl could want except…" Blushing, she turned away from him.

"Except what?" he asked.

"Um, are you going out with anyone special, Dan? Any significant other in your life?"

He'd never figure out how a woman's mind worked. Where had she pulled that question from?

"You've got to be kidding. I have no intention of getting involved with anyone, ever again. Do I look like a glutton for punishment?"

Silence greeted his reply, then a smile spread slowly across Alexis's face. "Truthfully, Dan, each time you take to the field, you're asking to be pummeled. So, my answer is yes. As in, yes, you're a glutton for punishment, all right." Her grin brightened further.

The woman was more than pretty. He itched to hug her, but didn't. "Well, well, well. Alexis Brown can joke when she wants to."

"Alexis Brown hasn't had much to laugh

about recently," said the woman who now stared at her niece. "And I never thought I'd have to relinquish all custody…." She shook her head, murmuring, "Sorry, Sherri."

The happy light in her eyes dimmed, but an angry heat rose inside him. She'd approached him, after all. It wasn't as though he'd asked for this responsibility. "Change the tune already, will ya? I'm tired of hearing it. I'm not the bad guy here," he bit out, and immediately regretted it. The woman was understandably upset.

She met his gaze, and he saw resignation. "You're not the bad guy at all. Any regrets I have, I brought on myself."

"What could you have done differently?"

"I don't know."

But he knew. The unthinkable idea had been lurking inside him since she'd shown up with his daughter. He'd questioned her about it once already, and she'd avoided givng him a direct answer.

"You could have kept Michelle away from me forever, and I'd never have known. But you didn't, because you needed money. You contacted me only because you were stuck for cash."

Her eyes blazed. "Is that what you really think? That money was my *only* motivation?"

Self-righteousness overflowed. Her explanation would be a doozy. "That's exactly what you told me. You said a little child support was all you needed, and that's almost a direct quote. What other reason could you have had, counselor?" He was baiting her, hoping for something more. For something more honorable.

"You stupid…stupid…athlete! All brawn, no brains." She walked toward him, looking ready to poke his eyes out with her extended pointer finger. She poked him in the chest instead.

"Cash flow may have been the immediate catalyst, but what would I have told Michelle when she grew up and asked about her daddy? When she asked me—the one person she would trust? Could I lie to her and say I didn't know who her father was?" She shook her head hard. "No. Lying is no way to raise a child, no way to build relationships."

Relief surged through him, and he was ready to divert her, but she was on a roll.

"Just as she has the right to know about her mother, Michelle also has the right to know her father. Every child wants to know their parents and deserves the truth. And if the truth stinks, it's still better than a bunch of lies."

He heard her breath come hard and short, as

though she was asthmatic. "Okay, okay, I believe you. Calm down."

"And how could I live with myself if I kept your identity a secret from her forever?"

Her tone, her body language, her outraged expression. It hadn't been simply happenstance that had brought his daughter to him. It had been this woman. She might have had her own timetable, but she'd taken the honest path.

"I believe you, Alexis. You did everything right and reasonable." He shrugged. "I apologize if I've insulted you. So, if you have no regrets, it's time to move on."

"Move on? Like you have?" she snapped. "Someone in this room is living in a glass house, and it's not me."

Her barbed arrow pierced his soul. He understood her meaning at once and resented it. Resented her. She had no right. She hadn't loved…she hadn't lost….

"Look, Michelle's waking up." Alexis stepped to the crib, their discussion forgotten, at least for the moment. He joined her in time to see his daughter's delight, her unabashed excitement, when she recognized her aunt.

When the baby laid her head on Alexis's shoulder and nuzzled, when he spotted the tears in Alexis's eyes, a shaky feeling hit the pit of his stomach. He was wrong. Alexis had loved and lost. Twice. Sisters count, too. His confidence wavered for the second time that afternoon. Alexis and Michelle loved each other. Was he doing the right thing?

If he weren't playing the next day, he would have reached for a drink.

The thought made him fidget. He touched his mouth, his leg. Couldn't relax. He looked at his daughter. Would he have really poured himself a glass? A wave of uncertainty shimmied through him. He didn't trust himself. His life was becoming as complicated as a playbook. A beer could become six too easily. He had new responsibilities now, and he couldn't afford to slip up.

CHAPTER FIVE

"MY FOLKS SHOULD BE here within the hour," said Dan, glancing at his watch the next morning, then at the door.

"We'll be fine. Go. The driver's waiting." Alexis couldn't hide her amusement. The big quarterback who made split-second decisions on a constant basis was pacing the hallway, first kissing the baby in Alexis's arms, then looking out the window at the car. Not sure where to go, or when.

"Thanks for coming over last night," he said for the third time. "Best night's sleep in three days."

"That was the whole point, wasn't it? Now, you can go win a game."

"Oh, yeah. That was the goal."

His wicked smile and gleaming eyes made her forget to breathe. She had to admit that her enemy was gorgeous—she'd thought so from the beginning. She was sure, however, the man with the powerhouse arm had no clue how powerful his smile could be.

"Winning is a lot more fun than losing." He was almost at the front door when he turned back to her again. "Everything should be normal tomorrow when the nanny comes. I won't have to ask for favors anymore."

Blinking herself back to reality, she flicked her hand in the air, brushing his remark away. "I'm very happy to spend time with Michelle. You should know that by now." She didn't care that her voice sounded hard. When it came to Michelle, there was no such thing as a favor. "And please let me know how your Mary Poppins works out tomorrow. I'd be more than happy to meet with her myself."

Without replying, he walked out and was gone.

"Well, he sure didn't seem to like that idea, did he, sweetheart?" she murmured to the baby. "But now I've got you all to myself and we can play."

Fifteen minutes later, their solitude was broken by a ringing doorbell. Leaving Michelle in her swing in the kitchen, Alexis ran to the door and opened it.

An older couple stood there—Dan's parents, she assumed—their arms filled with packages.

"Hi. I'm Alexis," she said, pasting a smile

on her face and opening the door wider. "Come on in."

But the couple didn't move. In fact, the blonde woman with the chic do simply stared at Alexis, eyes popping. She moved her mouth, but nothing came out. Then, she leaned against her husband and moaned. Alexis grabbed her packages. Dan's father reached for his wife, and his own bundles hit the floor.

The man glared at Alexis and, walking slowly, supported his wife to the living-room couch. "Get her some water," he barked.

The world had gone crazy, Alexis thought as she filled a glass. And if these loons thought for one minute she was leaving Michelle alone with them, they had another think coming. As for Dan? Just wait, Mr. Big Shot. She had a few words for him, too. Realizing she was trying to squeeze the glass she held, she forced her fingers to relax and reentered the living room.

Mrs. Delito was sitting up now, her husband beside her. Alexis offered her the water.

"What the hell is going on here? Who are you, really? And I expect a straight answer." Dan's father again, as he helped his wife hold the glass.

Had Dan not told his family anything? Alexis leveled a courtroom stare at the man. "Back off, Mr. Delito, so we can start from the beginning. Before your wife's fainting spell."

"She's not Kim." A soft voice from the couch. "She can't be." The woman made a pitiful attempt to smile at Alexis.

"She sure doesn't sound like Kim," said Mr. Delito. "Not with that attitude."

Good grief, thought Alexis, the pieces falling into place. These poor people had received a "good morning" they couldn't have foreseen in a million years because Dan hadn't warned them about her resemblance to his wife. None of which meant she'd leave the baby with them anyway.

"It seems," said Alexis, "that I'm a ringer for your late daughter-in-law. I'm so sorry for your shock, but sorrier that Dan didn't clue you in."

"Not as sorry as I am," said Dan's father, rising from the couch. "What could that boy be thinking, getting involved with you? First, the drinking, and now—" He threw his hands up in disgust, and with narrowed eyes, stared at Alexis again. "And now—some imitation wife."

Alexis, who'd survived much worse intimidation than this man could mete out, leaned forward and stared right back at him.

"My name is Alexis Brown, and you can bet your life that I'm no imitation. I'm my own woman." She looked him up and down. "When you find your manners again, I might allow you to play with your granddaughter—if you really care about her."

She walked from the room, leaving stunned silence behind her.

THE SMARTEST MOVE SHE'D made since contacting Dan was petitioning the court for visitation rights. She wouldn't depend on Dan's largesse or any ephemeral factor that might influence his mood. She needed to get Michelle out of this madhouse as often as possible.

Michelle had fallen asleep in the swing, and now Alexis lifted her out and walked past Dan's parents to the front stairs.

"Where are you taking her?" Dan's mother stood on the threshold of the living room, watching Alexis's progress with an anxious expression.

"Upstairs to the game room, where there's a crib. I'm going to hang out there, too, just until Dan gets home." She gave the woman her best smile and continued upstairs.

"You'll let us know when she wakes up, won't you?"

"Absolutely. Mrs. Delito, you'll be the first to know. In fact, you'll hear her through the intercom."

"That's right. I almost forgot about the intercom. We installed it when Kimmy was so sick."

The woman's lips quivered in her effort not to cry. Alexis had handled enough emotion for the morning, however, and simply waved and ran upstairs. No doubt, Kim had been an angel on earth. A perfect person. A perfect wife and daughter-in-law. But with no luck in the end. And Sherri? Not so perfect. Also with no luck in the end. Both were mourned. Both had been loved—one by many, one by few. But both had had much love to offer. And that, Alexis realized, was the common denominator.

As she settled Michelle for her nap, a wave of grief settled in her chest. Except for Dan during the initial meetings, everyone except Alexis had overlooked Sherri's existence. Dan's parents were caught up in themselves. They hadn't asked one question about Michelle's mom and seemed more consumed by the past than excited about the present or the future. Weren't they curious to learn about their grand-daughter's other family?

Once more, Alexis wondered if she'd made a dire mistake. *Sherri, did I misread you about contacting Dan Delito now? Have I done wrong here?*

Dan's parents joined her in the game room a half hour later, and small talk got them through the morning. When the game finally started at noon, Alexis sighed with relief. Three hours of mindless football would replace forced conversation and pointed questions, like the one Dan's father had asked five minutes ago.

"Didn't Danny say you could leave this morning after we showed up? Rita and I can take care of the baby."

I know you can, Alexis conceded. Despite their initial shock and hostility at Alexis's presence in the house, the Delitos had been nothing but kind to Michelle all morning. They were clearly as besotted with the baby as Dan was, which was encouraging. *Admit it, Brown. You don't want to leave Michelle with them because you don't want to leave her with anyone.* She simply smiled. "Sorry, but I don't recall." She focused on the in-home theater screen. "The game's about to start. How about relaxing with some Sunday-afternoon football?"

"A great idea," said Rita Delito. "Although I have to admit, I don't exactly relax watching my Danny on the field."

"She hides her eyes at the beginning of every play," said Nick, stroking his wife's shoulder. "Even when he was a kid, she couldn't watch."

"Really?" asked Alexis, amazed. "So why did you let him play?"

The couple glanced at each other and began to laugh. "Sorry, Ms. Brown," said Rita. "It wasn't a question of 'letting' him. He lived and breathed for the game from the moment he could hold the ball." Her brow crinkled as though she were still trying to solve a puzzle. "We'd never seen anything like it. Our older son, Joe, can play a mean piano, and Theresa can sing like a nightingale."

"But Danny," interrupted her husband, "he couldn't carry a tune on his back."

Strangely, when the conversation focused on Dan, Alexis started to enjoy herself. "I guess he wanted to feel special, too."

"You could be right."

The Dallas Cowboys were out for blood. By the end of the first half, Alexis was covering her eyes as much as Rita did.

"I bet he's not concentrating. Maybe he's thinking about the baby," Alexis said.

"Nope." Dan's father seemed sure of his response. "When you're staring at eleven guys weighing in at an average of 250 pounds, who are all out to get you, you don't think about anything else but football. His receivers aren't where they're supposed to be...."

"Well, they'd better shape up, or this little girl won't have a daddy!" The words popped out of Alexis without warning.

An awkward silence filled the room. Alexis glanced from one guest to the other.

"We're still getting used to that little fact," said Rita. "That Dan is a daddy. It's come as a bit of a shock, you know."

"Oh, I definitely know. I know all about shocks…like my sister's murder, for example." She let her words lie open for a moment. "Michelle's already lost her mother, so let's hope her father quits getting sacked during the second half."

She offered a tiny smile and, with surprise, watched Rita come over and knelt down on the play mat next to her and Michelle. "Both of you girls have suffered a major loss," Dan's mom said quietly, squeezing Alexis's hand. "I'm so sorry, Alexis."

"Thank you, Rita. Thank you very much." Maybe this emotional woman had a good heart underneath.

Nick's deep voice sounded behind them. "Is that where the baby gets her red hair? From her mother?"

"Sure does. You can thank Sherri for that strawberry-blond cap. But she might wind up with my eyes. A muddy hazel. Nothing to brag about."

The game on TV resumed, but Alexis's mind was elsewhere. The ice had been broken with these two important people. She'd put in a good day's work on Michelle's behalf.

Nick's shouts grabbed her attention. "Touchdown! Touchdown! Way to go, New England!" He punched his hands in the air and grinned at her. "They must have had some discussion in the locker room during halftime. Suddenly, everyone's where they should be, and if this keeps up, you know what that means?"

"Super—"

"Shush, shush," said Rita, actually putting her fingers over Alexis's mouth. "We don't speak that word out loud around here. Might jinx it, you know?"

Alexis looked from one supposedly sane adult to the other. She began to laugh and couldn't stop. They were all down the rabbit hole again. But this time, as crazy as it sounded, it was okay. They all got the joke, were on the same side. Maybe Dan's family really was loving and supportive and exactly what Michelle needed.

When the game ended with a win, Alexis got ready to leave. Rita knew her way around formula and diaper changes. The baby was napping again. Alexis's last bit of uneasiness evaporated.

She retrieved her belongings from the bedroom she'd used across the hall from Michelle, then stepped into the game room to say goodbye.

"Why are you leaving?" asked Nicky. "We're getting ready to party. The whole family's coming over. And Dan's friends. You'll never eat food this good anywhere else. You should stay."

What a difference an afternoon made. "Thanks, but not this time," Alexis replied with a smile. "I've got to get ready for work tomorrow. It's my first day back after my leave of absence. Can't afford to lose my job."

She brushed the baby's cheek with kisses, waved to Dan's parents and let herself out the front door. When she reached the corner, she paused. A party. Did that mean Dan would be drinking again? Unless she stayed, she'd never know. But surely the man wouldn't get blitzed in front of his parents. *Stop assuming the worst.* She'd seen him drunk only once, and he'd had a reason. She was overreacting, too sensitive. Placing once foot in front of the other, she continued on her way.

THE HOT SHOWER IN THE locker room didn't do it. He needed a long soak in a very hot tub. Every muscle in his body cried out for relief, but between the press interviews, the fans in the parking lot at Gillette and the traffic going home, it took Dan's driver over two hours to reach Chestnut Street.

Dan opened the door to a full house. Good. He scanned the room for his mom and the baby. Now, everyone would meet the latest addition to the family. He heard his name being called, and compliments on the rally in the second half. He waved to everyone.

"Where's my daughter?"

"Right here, Danny-boy. Right here." Theresa's voice.

His heart lightened as he beat a path to his sister, who held Michelle and was kissing her belly at the same time.

"Where's my little girl?" asked Dan softly when he stood next to her.

The baby's eyes opened wide, her arms and legs started their own dance, and Dan thought his heart would burst from his chest. "Come to Daddy, my little sweet pea," he cooed, taking Michelle from his sister.

He felt a kiss on his cheek, and a hug. "I don't know the details," said Theresa, "but I haven't seen you so calm and happy in too long. This baby is a good thing." She paused. "Oh, and congrats on the game. Well done. Of course, I always think any game in which you come out alive is a good one."

His parents appeared, and Nicky started to clap him on the shoulder.

"Easy, easy, Dad. I've got a delicate bundle here."

"Good job, son. Good job. A win at home and a new daughter. Perfect reasons for a party."

"I totally agree."

"Too bad Alexis didn't stay a little longer," said Nicky. "She could have met everyone."

"Alexis? Man, do I owe her. But I thought she would have left this morning after you and Mom showed up. That was the deal."

His dad's eyes narrowed. Furrows crossed his forehead. "She said she didn't remember any specific arrangement, so she stayed till the end of the game."

"Alexis not remember?" Dan's incredulity echoed in his voice. "She's got a memory like an elephant's, a steel trap. You can use any cliché you want, and that's her. She works for the D.A. She remembered, all right. She just didn't want to leave."

"Oh." The one soft syllable came from Rita. "Maybe because I fainted."

"Fainted? You?" What the hell had happened between his folks and Alexis during the day? Dan couldn't remember his mom ever fainting before.

"Your mother took one look at Alexis and passed out. And it's your fault, Danny-boy. You should have warned us."

He hoped insanity didn't run in the family, but he was beginning to wonder. "Warned you about what? She won't steal the silver."

Rita placed her palm against his forehead. "Do you have a fever? Or are you just blind?"

Now he got it. "Oh, I'm so sorry. I guess I forgot. I don't even notice the resemblance anymore. First of all, the eyes. Same big round eyes, but Alexis's are green, not brown, and a bit larger than Kim's. Her hair is a shade darker, too, and she's at least an inch taller—she comes up to here on me." He began to gesture, and Rita grabbed onto the baby.

"As if that's not enough difference—there's the personality. This one's a barracuda. While Kimmy…well, Kimmy was the gentlest person on the planet."

"My goodness, Dan. That was a lot of detail off the top of your head," said his mom.

He shrugged. "It's my job to notice details. How do you think we turned the game around?" He kissed his folks and ambled toward the eggplant parmigiana. The postgame meal was as important as the pregame meal the night before. He needed the correct balance of carbs, protein and good fats. And he needed hydration. He'd downed a bottle of sports drink with electrolytes while still at the stadium, but it wasn't enough liquid. He felt dry.

"Can I have a turn with her now, Danny?"

He smiled at Joe's wife, Mary Ann.

"I want her to meet all her cousins," his sister-in-law continued. She rose on tiptoe and kissed his cheek. "A heck of a beginning, but I know she's in good hands now."

Mary Ann whisked Michelle away, and a bottle of beer was placed in his hand. His friends were lifting their longnecks in a toast to him, and someone was saying lovely things about new lives and new beginnings.

The bottle was cool to the touch, the aroma tantalizing. A searing heat filled him. He felt beads of sweat pop out on his forehead. He wanted it.

Just one—to celebrate the win.

Just two—to celebrate the baby.

Just three—to celebrate. Anything.

Kim's image flashed; Alexis's image followed—like snapshots in his head. One worried; one disgusted.

"Dad! Joe!" His voice was strangled, but somehow the men of his family heard his call and were there. "I can't drink this. Take it away." The bottle disappeared.

"Water. I need water," Dan whispered.

He heard voices around him. Questions. His mom said something about dehydration upsetting a person's balance.

"Here you go, Danny-boy," said Nicky. "Juice. Water. Whatever you need. Drink as much as you want. We'll get rid of all the other stuff when we leave."

"Dad?"

"What, son?"

"Don't give up on me."

CHAPTER SIX

BY TEN O'CLOCK THE next morning, Alexis was buried under a dozen case files she'd found waiting for her on her desk. Greetings of "welcome back" were superseded only by "Thank God you're back." Nevertheless, it was nice to be appreciated, and she dived into her work with rekindled enthusiasm.

Not that she forgot about Michelle. Her apartment held a repository of memories, and the baby sat in the back of her mind all the time. She'd run out of the condo that morning as though being chased by a swarm of bees.

Maybe she'd call Roz later and see if she was free for dinner. The other woman was single, too. They'd meet as friends, not as social worker to client. Alexis needed a friend. In fact, she needed more than one if she were to fill up her hours after work and avoid the empty apartment. Now would be a good time to build a social life—or at least try. She'd make the effort, be caring, share ideas—even if they led to personal discussions. Or maybe she'd join a book club. That seemed safer.

Her cell rang an hour later. She'd barely identified herself when Dan's voice came through. No hello. No greeting of any kind.

"The first Mary Poppins didn't show. She's no longer available. The second one was horrible, and I sent her packing. The third one looked like she was twelve years old. No way."

She heard his stress and tried to calm him. "Appearance doesn't matter. She might be very qualified."

"Her tongue was pierced. She had four earrings in each ear. Need I say more?"

Now Alexis began to pace. "What about a good day care?"

"I need night and weekend people, too. I'm out of town a lot. Besides, there's the question of security. I'm rich and famous. Yippee."

He sounded miserable.

"Do you want me to stay over tonight? I can stop at my apartment first…."

"Yes," he said, drawing out the one syllable into five. "But not just tonight. I've been thinking, Alexis. Thinking about the situation a lot. You're the best Mary Poppins the baby

could have. I want you to come here full-time.
I'll cover whatever you're earning in the D.A.'s
office plus a good bonus."

The breath whooshed out of her lungs.
"Would you mind repeating that? I'm not sure
I understand."

"I'm offering you the job."

When he explained again, she listened hard,
clasping her phone in a viselike grip. "You sure
know how to turn my world upside down." Her
scrambled brain burst with one thought after
another, all tumbling over themselves. She had
to consider the negatives.

"Before we discuss this further," she began,
"we have to clear something up."

"You'd be perfectly safe here! I'd never take
advantage of you, never."

Stunned, she remained silent because that
possibility hadn't crossed her mind. She'd
never felt threatened in all the times she'd been
with him. Not even that first time, when he was
loaded. She could handle loaded.

Maybe she was being naive. After all, he was
a healthy male. She was a healthy female. She
should have thought of complications. But then
she remembered all the times he spoke about
Kim, his love and gentleness apparent.

"Thanks, Dan, but that wasn't my point. You

need to know right up front that I petitioned the probate court for legal access to Michelle. That means court-decreed visitation rights. In the beginning, I had hoped for joint custody, but… well, that didn't happen. And as for the visits— you had been a bit vague about that, and I couldn't trust you."

A low whistle came through the phone. "You're sure being 'up-front,'" he said. "It's not every day I'm called a liar."

She winced. She'd challenge a statement like that, too. "Let's just say I'd trust you with my life, but not with my heart. We're talking about Michelle, and that little baby *is* my heart. So, I don't trust that part of you. I have to fight for my rights, and I will. The court won't ignore Sherri's family…the mother's family."

"Tell me what you think is fair, and I'll have Andy draw up an agreement."

He'd surprised her again. "Just like that?" she asked, snapping her fingers although he couldn't see the gesture or hear the noise. "That's a total about-face from earlier conversations."

"A week ago, taking care of Michelle was a plan. A concept. It wasn't real. Sort of like a new football play when it's still on paper. It's different when you actually try it out. A lot harder."

Well, he was learning. Michelle wasn't a theory. She was reality with a capital *R*.

"When my wife was sick," he continued, "I made sure she had the best care possible. Why would I do less for my daughter?"

Whoa. Now he was calling her the "best"?

"Nice try, but flattery won't get you anywhere. I'm no nanny icon. Whatever I know, I've learned in four months. And I don't know everything."

"I'm not worried about you! Look, Alexis, I'm asking, pleading, begging, call it anything you want. Stay with us until the season's over, then you'll have your visits. All written down and legal. And besides," he added softly, "don't you want to do what's best for Michelle?"

O-o-h, the man was crafty. "Of course I want what's best for the baby." If she went along with his plan, she'd be doing it not only for Michelle, but for Sherri's sake, too. And for herself. Maybe to silence her own conscience. So many regrets… so many unknowns.

She looked at her overflowing desk. At her coworkers passing by. At the door to her boss's office. She winced. He'd been so glad to see her that morning.

"I'd never planned to leave my job, Dan, and now I'll lose it. I've used up my leave of absence."

"I'll also cover your salary afterward—for however long it takes you to find another position. Let's see…how else can I entice you?

"You won't have to do a thing in the house. I have a cleaning service twice a month. And Maria comes in two mornings a week to handle the kitchen and food prep."

Apparently Dan was quite used to spending his way out of every problem. Was she another convenient service he could buy? *Be fair,* Alexis told herself. *He tried to hire a nanny but rejected the idea in the end. And hiring me would be more than a financial transaction.* She squeezed her eyes shut. *Don't let your suspicions get in the way of what's best for Michelle. She'll thrive with her auntie here to care for her and love her.*

No one could take away her license to practice law; later, she could reapply with the Suffolk County D.A. or any D.A.'s office in the state. She could consider private law firms or nonprofits who needed lawyers on staff. Now more comfortable with her employability factor, she tuned in to Dan once more. She must have remained quiet for too long, however, because Dan started selling again.

"I'll be away a lot of the time. Not just on the road for games, but we have daily practices at the stadium, we review videos constantly, we develop strategies, we train—all of that is critically important. You might not believe it, but playing on an NFL team is a full-time job."

She'd made up her mind to do it, but now she wanted him to work a little harder closing the sale. Payback, maybe?

"Most adults have full-time jobs, Dan. And plenty of people take business trips."

"Whew, you sound like my family, putting me in my place. No swelled heads allowed. So—I'm holding my breath here—will you live with us for three months?"

"You know what's really ironic, Dan?"

"No-o-o, but your voice sounds happy."

"I've worked so hard to get my diplomas—eleven years altogether. And now, after all that, I'm going to have 'full-time nanny' on my résumé. It's unbelievable."

His deep laughter joined her light chuckle. "An excellent choice. Thank you. You're a lifesaver."

"Oh, let's just say I like a guy who begs."

"THE CHOICE IS YOURS," said Dan with a suitcase in each hand as he led Alexis inside his house. "There's a guest suite on the top floor, complete with its own bathroom, a study and a terrace overlooking the neighborhood. Or there's the room you used on Saturday night, across from Michelle."

"I'm not a guest, Dan. I'm part of the household. And naturally, I'd rather be close to Michelle."

Just what he wanted to hear. "Great. Walk or ride?"

"Ride? What do you mean?"

He led them to a narrow door, pressed a button on the wall and the door slid open. The snug elevator held them with one of the suitcases as they rode to the third floor.

"You sure have a lot of amenities."

"This one comes in very handy, like now, when you're holding the baby. It's safer than two flights of stairs."

The elevator door opened, and Dan continued the tour. "In case you didn't notice the other night, the three bedrooms are all here," he said. "Mine's at the front of the house and you two are at the back. You'll have your own bathroom."

"I remember."

He followed Alexis to the bedroom that would be hers and watched her absorb the surroundings. He would have just plopped on the bed or thrown his belongings down. But he'd been married long enough to know women were different, that Alexis would probably look around, touch things, organize herself. He also knew Alexis would probably like the room. Kim had had a flair for decorating and had given her attention to every room in the house. He watched as Alexis fulfilled his expectations and perused the place with interest.

"I didn't take the time to notice anything when I was here before, but it's pretty, Dan. I like the soft colors, the curtains and spread. The bookshelves are handy, and the corner desk is perfect for my laptop. It'll work out fine for a few months."

"If you need anything at all, just ask. I want you to treat the place—the whole place—as your own. I don't want the new nanny to quit."

Michelle started to squirm and cry. "Let me have her," said Dan. "You're probably tired after a full day's work."

"Not tired at all," replied Alexis. "I used to work out regularly at a fitness club in the evenings—before Michelle came into my life."

"Oh, okay. It's just that Kim's mind was stronger than her body, and I... Oh, never mind." Why couldn't he keep his mouth shut? Alexis didn't want to hear about his past.

"Dan?"

He glanced at her.

"The baby needs a diaper change."

And they needed a change of subject, as well. Michelle had good timing.

"She's stinky," said Alexis. "That's what the squirming and crying were all about."

No problem. Nannies changed diapers. "You know where her room is." He pointed across the hall.

"Do you think she'll be toilet trained in three months when I leave? It's time for *Daddy* to step up to the plate."

"The plate? Wrong game, *Auntie*."

She rolled her eyes. Laughing, he said, "Cute, Alexis, cute." He reached for the baby, and they went to her room. Laying Michelle on the changing table, he started chatting to her as Alexis had suggested that day in her condo. "Let's get you nice and clean."

After disposing of the soiled diaper, he slipped a clean one under his daughter. "Now I need the butt paste," he murmured to himself.

He awkwardly tidied his daughter with a couple of baby wipes, then found the powder and cream and applied both liberally. He'd just fastened one side of the diaper when he sensed Alexis behind him. "Want any help?" she asked, peering around his shoulder.

Before he could answer, she stepped closer.

"Holy Toledo, Dan! The diaper's too loose. She'll soak through everything. Close it tighter, like this," she said, demonstrating with the tabs.

"No wonder the laundry's piled up," he said. "But practice is something I know how to do." He dived into diaper action once more. "I learned all about car seats, so I can learn all about diapers." When he finished, he turned to his new mentor. "Satisfied, Coach?"

Her warm smile reached her eyes, and he found his gaze lingering.

"Oh, I like that new title," she said. "But beware, I'm tough."

"Nothing I can't handle," Dan replied, then wanted to cut his tongue out. Sexual banter wasn't part of the deal. He waited for her reaction, but she didn't pick up on the remark. On purpose or not?

"Four months ago," Alexis said, taking the baby from him, "I needed a coach myself. Roz came in handy."

"It must have been tough…with everything else."

She nodded. "There was no one else to help. I don't have a relationship with my parents. Cal's been an alcoholic all his adult life, and Peggy's an enabler. Sherri and I got out as soon as possible."

"Speaking of which," he said, "there's no alcohol in the house anymore."

Her gaze jumped to his and held.

"You saw me at my worst," he continued, confident in the truth of every word, "so, if you're concerned at all, you don't have to be. I'm done with it."

She touched him, and his arm burned. "After watching you play, and getting to know you better, it's barely entered my mind lately," she said in a quiet tone. "But frankly, if there's any hint of alcohol use, then neither Michelle nor I can count on being safe with you."

She moved slightly, her hand dropping to her side. His skin cooled immediately; he preferred the heat. "Michelle not being safe is unacceptable—at any price," she added.

"I agree. And I appreciate your trust."

"Oh, you're still earning that, but you get points for trying to be a good daddy."

Her green eyes seared his. "I'm familiar with the empty promises of alcoholics, with their rationalizations and their blaming others for everything wrong in their lives. I've seen the damage caused by their out-of-control behavior. If you've got a real problem, Dan, I'll know about it, and I'll be able to protect Michelle." She waved her arm, lightening the atmosphere. "I'm known to be a pretty good judge of character, and my money's on you. Just don't prove me wrong this time."

THE NEXT MORNING, ALEXIS watched in amazement as Dan built his breakfast in a soup bowl. Two types of multigrain cereal, fresh blueberries, a sliced banana, a half-dozen strawberries and an avalanche of milk. The man needed a tureen, not a bowl.

He raised his head. "What's the matter?"

"Uh, nothing. It's a colorful volcano…for about three people."

Grinning, he pushed the bowl toward her. "Help yourself."

"Eat up. Michelle needs a healthy daddy."

It was almost nine o'clock, and her morning had been filled with Michelle-centered activities, including laundry—which hadn't been done since the baby moved in last Thursday. The elevator had proved handy for getting to the machines in the basement.

"Maria should be here any minute. I want to introduce you before I leave."

"The kitchen person?"

"Just call her General. We do. She stayed here a lot when Kim was sick, acting like a general at a command center, and now she comes in two mornings a week. She orders groceries, prepares and freezes dinners for me. Just write down what you want and she'll add it to the list. No problem."

"I don't want to cause the woman more work. I'll shop for myself."

"Don't be ridiculous. She uses my credit card and mostly shops online. The stuff is delivered. There's no extra work."

Alexis simply stared at him. "Wow. I guess the rich really are different."

Dan leaned back in his chair. "We bleed red, just like the rest of humanity. Get used to it, because I'm giving you card access, as well. You buy whatever you think Michelle needs for now. When the season's over, I'll have more time—"

The sound of the doorbell was followed by a woman's voice calling Dan's name. Footsteps approached and Maria Sanchez entered the kitchen, took one look at Alexis and made the sign of the cross.

"Madre de Dios," she said, grabbing onto a chair back.

"Here we go again," mumbled Alexis. "I swear I'm going blonde and getting a haircut."

"No, don't do that," Dan said, quickly going to Maria. "I like you just the way you are."

Why did that remark make her feel so good?

She watched him lean over and explain her presence to Maria, saw that words weren't necessary after the woman spotted Michelle. Joy radiated from every part of her.

"Such a beautiful baby! Señor Daniel, now you get happy again. No?"

He hugged her, then stood up, dwarfing the five-foot-zero-inch woman. "Yes, Maria. I'll be happy again." But his gaze traveled to Alexis, and he inclined his head.

His salute of thanks was easy to read, and she nodded in return. Maybe, just maybe, contacting Dan had been the smartest move she'd ever made.

Now, Dan pointed at Alexis and then at a sheet of paper on the table. "I made of list of phone numbers—my folks, the store, the cell numbers, Joe's, Theresa's, my coach, Gillette Stadium… In an emergency, you call any of them. Or my friend, Andy Romano. You've met him."

She loved it when he tried so hard, loved it because he reinforced her decision to contact him. She'd done the right thing. "I know half the cops in the city. In a real emergency, we're covered," she told him. "Relax. Go to work. Knock yourself out…ooh, not really."

"Enough with the jokes," he said, grinning. "I'm trying to tell you both something. Something important."

Alexis glanced at Maria and shrugged. The woman shrugged back.

"Management's moving forward," said Dan. "Thursday's paper will contain a small paragraph about Michelle being my daughter. We have no choice but to break the news, or the tabloids will catch on sooner or later and turn the story on its head."

He was right. This wasn't a joke. Alexis's muscles tightened, tension filled her. "What are you expecting afterward? A load of paparazzi on the doorstep?"

"Hopefully not, but you never know what the gossip rags will do. We have a good rapport with the mainstream media, so I'm not concerned about them. Just don't open the door to anyone for a couple of days after the article appears."

"Not a problem. Michelle and I will take some nice long walks today and tomorrow. Maybe we'll go to the Public Gardens."

"Make way for ducklings," sang Dan, with an envious smile.

He looked as though he wanted to join them, and Alexis squeezed his hand. "When the season's over, Danny, you'll have time for walks, you'll have the baby all to yourself and the ducklings will make way for you!"

He seemed surprised, as though he'd forgotten about later on. "I will, won't I?" He gave her a quick kiss on the forehead, grabbed his gym bag and left for the stadium.

"He's a good man, my Señor Daniel, no?" Maria asked, not hiding her curiosity.

"He's a good man, Maria, but get that look out of your eye. He's Kim's man, not mine. And besides, I don't want to live in Manderley."

The woman frowned.

"I meant, this is also Kim's house. Her presence is everywhere. I'm only a visitor, Michelle's aunt. La tia Alexis. And that's all."

Maria shook her head, broke into a babble of Spanish that Alexis couldn't follow and began taking an inventory of the fridge.

Alexis took the baby and made her escape.

THE BOSTON GLOBE—SPORTS
Thursday, November 1
QUARTERBACK DAN DELITO
FATHER OF BABY GIRL
After proving paternity through DNA testing, Dan Delito was granted full custody of a baby girl through the probate court last week. The baby's mother is deceased, a victim of foul play, according to police reports. "No one can take the place of a mother," said Delito. "But my daughter

will be surrounded by a big, loving family
with lots of cousins to play with."

SITTING AT THE KITCHEN TABLE, already dressed
for the day, Alexis folded back the morning
paper and circled the article. If Dan hadn't
alerted her in advance, she would have missed
the story. It was a short piece buried at the
bottom of the NFL page.

She sensed Dan behind her and pointed it
out. "I almost didn't see it. Maybe no one else
will, either."

"Fat chance." He began assembling his
morning feast.

Maria hustled over—Tuesday and Thursday
were her days—and Alexis showed it to her.
"Have you seen this yet?"

"*Si.* I always read *futbol* news." The woman
shrugged. "The beautiful baby is here. Is Dan's
and that's good." But her voice seemed unsure,
and Alexis probed.

"What's the matter, Maria?"

The woman waved toward the front of the
house. "I have fear."

Dan rose from his seat. "You're safe here,
Maria."

"*Hay caramba!*" The housekeeper turned to
Alexis. "Just like last time with Mrs. Kim.

People, writers, photographers, they all come to the house. They wait outside." She shook her head. "They want to talk, take pictures. Pictures? Of a sick lady? Of my poor Daniel? No! Is no good, all those people. No good."

Wow. Maria had made herself heard, and Alexis was taking mental notes. No one wanted to be stalked.

"It was a very small article," Alexis said with authority, "in the middle of the week. Not even after a game. I'm sure no one will see it."

Maria shook her head. "One person reads, then says to the next to the next. People talk. You will see." Whispering to herself and clucking her tongue, Maria opened the pantry door, then turned to Dan again.

"You got calories for a flan today? I bake."

"Sure," he boomed. "Lots of calories to spare."

Surprised at his volume, Alexis peered at Dan. He was putting on a show. Hugging Maria. Smiling wide.

Alexis had already learned the man was disciplined with food. He lived on certain amounts of carbs, proteins and fats. Maria's delicious creamy dessert would be loaded with fat, cholesterol and calories. He was taking the gas pipe for the sake of a woman who'd been loyal during the hardest times in his life.

"I happen to love flan," Alexis said. "Believe me, it won't go to waste."

The woman glowed.

The man grinned—directly at her.

Alexis blushed, felt her face flame. She quickly turned her head and scooped the baby from her play mat. "Time to go for a nice long walk, sweetheart, but—phew—you're stinky again. Back upstairs we go."

Dan was waiting when they returned. "I've got a little time. I thought I'd join you for a couple of blocks, then walk to my car. You'd be on your own afterward."

"Sure," said Alexis, "I'll even let you push the stroller."

"Great. I'm going to call your bluff on that." He leaned over Michelle. "Want Daddy to push you, baby?"

Michelle's eyes drifted closed, and Dan's carefree laughter floated in the air. A musical sound that made Alexis smile.

"The ladies in my life sure know how to take me down a peg."

Boston's star quarterback could laugh at himself—a nice trait. It seemed there was a whole lot more to Dan Delito that Alexis had yet to discover.

IN FIVE MINUTES, THEY were outside, enjoying the crisp, fresh air. Dan took a deep breath. Maybe it was because of the game and his career, but fall had always been his favorite season. Nothing beat the blazing foliage of a New England autumn, the expanse of apple orchards loaded with red and yellow fruit, or roadside stands filled with plump orange pumpkins and other gourds. Now, a pale sun made an appearance with a promise of more warmth later on. Dan reached for the stroller, eager to try out a new daddy chore.

"You look like the Cheshire cat," said Alexis.

"I'm grinning like a happy man." It actually felt strange. He hadn't felt happy in years. He emitted a long, low whistle as the thought hit him. He hadn't wrestled with his grief in a little while. Could a baby do all that? Was his adorable daughter the key to a happy future? Was it because Alexis was part of the picture? If nothing else, the challenging woman had jolted him from his ennui.

He automatically set a fast pace, but Alexis was right beside him. "You okay?"

"Loving it. Remember, I'm Boston's most loyal walker, but slow down on the cobblestones for Michelle's sake."

"Absolutely."

"How come you're driving yourself today?"

"I like driving, but not on game day or on airport treks for away games. Louis is my usual driver. You'll meet him on Sunday after we beat Miami."

"Sunday?"

"Sure. We're playing at home again. The whole family's going—they always do. You and Michelle, too. We all chipped in for a reserve box at Gillette. No one wanted to be left out."

"I can watch on TV," she quickly replied. "Your mom and dad can take the baby. I trust them. Rita can change a mean diaper."

Her immediate protest caught him by surprise. Most people would give their eyeteeth for a box view at the stadium. But nothing was simple with Alexis or their entire situation.

He eyed her closely—puckered brow, tight mouth—a picture of worry. He softly said, "No one's going to faint this time, and I'd like the rest of my family to meet you."

Silence.

"You're very important."

More silence.

"I don't even see the resemblance anymore."

"Liar."

He rattled off the list of differences he'd once shared with his mother.

"Good Lord, Dan, have you examined me in a petri dish?"

He chuckled, wrapped an arm around her and pulled her close. "But you *are* different, Alexis. Totally unique."

She fit perfectly against him. More important, she felt wonderful against him. A long time had passed since he'd had his arms around a woman—at least when he was stone-cold sober. Two years to be exact.

It was easy with Alexis, almost too easy, and that gave him pause. He never trusted anything that was too easy.

CHAPTER SEVEN

A "BOX" DIDN'T ADEQUATELY describe the Delitos' thousand-square-foot luxury suite at the stadium. Beautiful furnishings, a private bar and private restrooms delineated the space overlooking the field. More overwhelming to Alexis than her surroundings, however, was the family horde.

Maybe a hundred people, big and little, approached all at once. At least, it *seemed* like a hundred to Alexis, but maybe it was fifty. She'd never liked crowds, so, pasting a smile on her face, she braced herself for the onslaught of…maybe…twenty-five squealing kids and curious adults anxious to get their hands on Michelle.

A man approached first, looking just like Dan, but heftier.

"Hi, Alexis. I'm Joe Delito, Danny's big brother and manager of Delito's Italian Deli and Market."

Shaking his hand, she tilted her head back to look him in the eye, then stole a glance at his petite mother. Joe followed her gaze.

"Wow," said Alexis. "It's a good thing babies grow afterward."

Joe's hearty laughter rang out. "Good point."

"So, why aren't you on the field, too?"

"No regrets there. I played in school—defensive line—but to me, it was only a game. For Dan, it's his passion. Although," he continued as he reached for the baby, "he seems to have found another passion."

"Ooh, she's gorgeous!" A woman's voice. "My turn, Joe. My turn."

Alexis met Mary Ann, Joe's wife, and their three young sons. Then Dan's sister, Theresa, needed a turn with Michelle. She nuzzled the infant as though she'd never let go.

"Larry and I have three kids, also," she said, waving one arm around the suite. "Three girls, but in this family, there's always room for more. I'm so glad you called Dan. We're all thrilled to have a new niece."

No one fainted. Alexis couldn't fault any of them for their behavior. Dan must have threatened them with expulsion from the suite; Rita and Nick must have threatened to withhold the baby from visits.

More people came. Two young single cousins, then Andy Romano and his family, and Louis Gates—Dan's driver, who said he'd be taking her and Michelle home that night with Dan.

"Sorry I can't drive you, but it's a late game," said Nicky. "I have to open the store early tomorrow."

"What about the car seat?" she protested, thinking about the time it had taken earlier to load Nick's car with the baby's paraphernalia and install the seat. They'd been lucky to arrive at the stadium before kickoff.

"Nick and I will handle that at halftime. Not to worry," said the chauffeur with a smile, a handshake and a piercing stare as though memorizing her features for later recall. "I've been driving Mr. Delito around for a long time, and now that he's a dad, I'll take even better care of him."

She wondered if he was referring to late nights at a club or if he'd simply made an innocent remark about getting the star QB to the airport on time. Her stomach tightened when she thought about the first option. She hoped she never had cause to investigate Dan's whereabouts.

She had no time left to wonder. Miami had won the coin toss and chosen to receive, and the game was in play. She relaxed. The Patriots' defensive line was on duty. Dan was safely on the sidelines for a little while.

Miami's aggressive offensive line completed two downs in five minutes and were driving for a TD. Cameras roved to a grim Dan, watching from his seat. The crowd was roaring for defense, not an auspicious beginning to a home game. In the suite, Alexis heard mumblings and quiet swears. Miami had scored.

"Oh, God," Rita whispered, "they'll want to keep their lead. When we're in possession, they're gonna take Dan out right after the snap."

"The correct word is *try,* Rita. They're gonna try to take him out." Nick didn't look as confident as his words sounded.

Whatever. Alexis didn't blink. She put on her cop face. This game was exactly like every other game, and Dan was always in danger.

"You don't seem too concerned," said Joe. "That's good. Enjoy the game."

She shrugged. "You said it first. It's his passion. His choice. I'm not getting emotional about a stupid game." But her heart began to race, and her hands were damp. With the stealth of a shadow, fear had made its presence known. She was angry with herself for caring, and with Dan for choosing such a dangerous sport.

"In fact, Joe, I'm not going to watch," she

said. "And Michelle's not going to watch, either. How does your mother survive?"

Without waiting for an answer, she picked up the baby. "Let's go find your little cousins and play."

"Ostrich," Joe teased.

Ignoring him, she scanned the room and approached a lively group of boys and girls, the oldest maybe eight or nine.

She didn't have to say a word before she was surrounded.

"Michelle wants to say hi." Alexis waved the baby's arm at the kids.

"Can I hold her?" asked Emily. Or was it Elizabeth? Both had dark eyes and identical ponytails. Sisters for sure. An adorable toddler girl stood next to them. Theresa and Larry's kids, she surmised.

"Let's all sit down on the floor," Alexis began. The little girls obliged immediately. The little boys just stood there. "Hi, Michelle," one said. "Gotta watch the game. See you later." A small boy chorus echoed his sentiments.

Alexis saluted. "Gotcha. Go have fun." She joined the girls on the floor and plopped Michelle on her lap. "Who's first to hold Michelle?"

The tallest girl, Elizabeth, answered immediately, and Alexis carefully put Michelle into her big cousin's lap.

The middle sister, Emily, tapped Alexis on the arm. "I know who you really are," she whispered. "You're Auntie Kim's angel. Aren't you?"

"Um…" Her voice trailed away. Obviously, no one had clued the kids in about the resemblance. And now she had to handle a loaded question. When Alexis was a kid, Sherri used to ask her impossible questions, too, her nose wrinkled in confusion as she waited for logical answers from her big sister. Half the time, Alexis invented the answers, but Sherri had needed to believe her and been satisfied. Alexis wondered if she still had a working imagination.

The little girls waited as Alexis slowly looked from one to the other. "If I were an angel, I'd have wings to fly with, and I'd fly around the football field helping Uncle Danny. Just like that." She snapped her fingers. "But, look," she said, standing up again and turning around. "Nothing. No wings. I have to walk step by step, just like you and everyone else."

"See! I told you so." Elizabeth frowned but hugged the baby. "She's not Auntie Kim's angel. She's just a regular person."

"But maybe—" the younger girl tugged Alexis's hand "—maybe you just don't got your wings yet. You gotta *earn* them, you know, just like Clarence did."

Clarence. Shades of *It's A Wonderful Life.*

The older girl was paying attention again, and Alexis wished she could think of a brilliant response, one that would satisfy these sensitive children. She didn't have a clue.

Theresa's voice chimed in at that moment, and Alexis sagged with relief. "I see five beautiful angels in front of me." She pointed at each of the four girls, including Michelle, and then at the adult. Her gaze met Alexis's in a warm expression of what could only be sincere gratitude. "In my book, you *are* an angel—for bringing Michelle to us. She is exactly what Danny needs—and you're not such bad medicine, either."

"Should have watched the darn game," mumbled Alexis, avoiding Theresa's glance. "I'm being sacked too many times myself."

THE MIAMI DOLPHINS WERE kicking their butts. Particularly Dan's. Their defense was all over him like cheese on a pizza. He'd barely caught the snap before they brought him down right in the pocket. Where were his guards? Overwhelmed, too. He had no time to set up a pass to his receivers. Sure, Miami wanted the win, wanted it bad. The two AFC teams were tied for the season so far with nine wins and one loss. Neither of them wanted a second loss.

But one would earn it.

Dan's team was down by seven, the score 28–21 with three minutes left in the game. By now, he knew he'd need an extra moment to scan the defense before passing, because the Dolphins were taking him out every damn time. He was tired of the slew of bodies on top of him. He didn't want to go home limping again. Alexis already thought football was a dumb game.

They'd made a first down and were going for their second. On the thirty-seven-yard line, he signaled his center and guards for a shotgun offense, rarely used, and then placed himself six yards back to receive the snap. If his teammates were surprised, they kept it hidden. He'd studied his playbook, he'd reviewed hundreds and hundreds of hours of videos, he'd studied the offense, the defense, every nuance of the game, and he'd studied the pros from yesterday and today. Pictures stayed in his head. Now, he saw John Elway of the Denver Broncos, who'd been an expert in shotgun offense.

Dan took his place, his center snapped to him and, in what felt like slow motion, he caught the ball, scanned the Dolphins' defense and spotted his receiver. He threw the ball in a straight line toward Al Tucker, who ran on an angle to meet it. Tuck jumped, caught it and drove toward the goal, three Dolphins after him.

Touchdown!

The screams of the hometown crowd filled the stadium. In his own world, Dan heard nothing. His eyes told him that his strategy had worked.

Six points earned, and now they were only one point behind. The Patriots' special team kicker got ready for the point-after kick. And made it.

Tied score at twenty-eight.

In the suite, Alexis held the baby while Nicky, Rita and the entire family jumped and cheered, screaming like the crazed fans in the bleachers.

"Only a minute and a half left," said Nicky. "They'll go into overtime."

"More chance for him to get killed," Alexis said. "In fact, I'm surprised his wife didn't mind. I read that the damage to a person's body playing one game is the equivalent of being in an auto accident."

Rita came over and patted her shoulder. "Who knows what will happen in life? In the end, it was Kim who was taken, no football involved. She often said that Dan's high energy perked her up and made her feel safe." Then she hugged Alexis. "But it's nice to see that you're concerned for him. You're a lovely woman, Alexis. We like you."

An odd thing to say. "Well, thanks. I hope you'll still feel that way when my nanny stint is over. Michelle is…well, she's the only real family I've got." It was true. She hadn't seen or heard from her parents since Sherri's death, which was fine with her. They all lived in the same city but in different worlds.

"You're the baby's aunt, Alexis. You're part of our family now, just like Michelle is," said Nicky. "And that's a fact."

Maybe. Maybe not.

"Overtime's starting," Joe called out.

She scanned the room for Andy Romano. Reminding him about drafting the visitation arrangements couldn't hurt.

LUCK WAS WITH NEW ENGLAND. The Patriots won the coin toss and had the first crack at scoring in overtime. Their offense took the field, including Dan Delito. Eleven determined opponents would do everything in their power to stop him from scoring.

Alexis's nails bit into her palms. In her imagination, the baby could wind up with no father at all.

After two minutes of play, however, New

England drove the ball far enough downfield to try for a field goal. The field goal kicker kicked. The ball flew between the goalposts and the game was over. A sudden-death victory by three points.

Alexis went limp with relief. At this rate, she wouldn't last through the season.

"Dan's in the press box," Nicky said a few minutes later.

She turned toward the jumbo screen to watch and listen.

"It was a tough, man-to-man game," said Dan into the camera. "Miami is a great team." He stood on the sidelines, helmet under his arm, microphone in his face.

"He looks good," said Rita, eyes glued to the screen. "Dirt doesn't count. He walked evenly, his eyes are focused…."

Seemed like Rita did her own play-by-play after each game.

Dan continued. "A tough contest—we're all breathing hard—but it turned out right, at least for New England." He grinned into the camera.

"What about that shotgun offense at the end of regulation?" asked the commentator.

"When it's life or death, sometimes you can't stick to the script. You've gotta rewrite it. That's my job. In fact," he said, "I'm going to do it again. Right now."

He raised his helmet. "Here's to Michelle and Ally, a couple of new fans."

The announcer chuckled and thanked his guest. Dan waved at the camera again and trotted to the locker room.

Alexis sat openmouthed in the suite. Ally? What was that all about?

"You know something?" asked Rita. "I think his new fans are doing him a world of good."

But at what cost to herself? Alexis looked at the crowd in the suite, then glanced back at the emptying field, her stomach cramping as all the changes in her life crashed down on her simultaneously. Protecting Michelle. Quitting her job. Dealing with too many new people. Deciphering relationships. Rubbing shoulders with the NFL. Missing her conversations with Roz, the new friend who'd seen her through the worst time of her life. They'd never had that dinner....

Scariest of all for Alexis, however, was finding herself attracted to Michelle's dad, a man who still yearned for his late wife. A man whose only interest now was his daughter.

GULPING FROM HIS water bottle, Dan walked out of the locker room into the night an hour after game's end, knowing he'd be soaking his sore muscles in his home spa later on. The entire team would be back on the field by noon tomorrow to start their weekly reconditioning process and to review videos of today's game, especially the first half, when they'd trailed the Dolphins.

He peered ahead, trying to spot the limo, wondering where the normally reliable Louis was, while at the same time waving to fans who'd remained to greet him. A lot of fans. It seemed like hundreds.

"Great job, Dan!"

"Whaddayathink about the Super Bowl? Any chance?"

Wincing at that one, he kept waving and smiling.

"Hey, Dan. How's fatherhood?"

He almost stopped to answer but thought better of it and just called over his shoulder. "Fantastic. I love it. She's gorgeous."

Whoops and hollers followed that, some cheers and applause. With all his concern about paparazzi and gossip sheets, he hadn't realized he'd also receive some public support. Interesting. And gratifying.

He finally spotted the limo. Actually, he spotted Louis waving both arms up and down as if he were making vertical snow angels. Dan jogged over and received a huge clap on the back. Rather unusual for the driver—a handshake was more in order—but everyone loved a winning team. Why should Louis be an exception?

"Mr. Delito, we have special company tonight." The man opened the back door with a flourish, and there were Alexis and Michelle.

Warmth filled him, a warmth that had nothing to do with the game or the win or the cheering crowd. He gave Louis a thumbs-up and could feel a smile cross his face as he got into the car and sat next to his passengers on the wide seat.

"What a great surprise."

"I hope so. Your dad's idea, to save him the extra driving. He has to open the store early tomorrow. I didn't see a reason to refuse, but I don't want to intrude on your privacy, either."

"Intrude? Never." But Dan smelled a setup arranged by his dad and carried out by his chauffeur. Extra driving? His folks lived less than five miles from him. And Nicky always gave him a bear hug after a game. Dan wanted to laugh.

The baby was awake, trying to eat a rattle. He peeked in at her and whispered her name. She waved her arms wildly, excited at seeing him. Who knew being a daddy would be this wonderful? Who knew that one grin from this baby could melt 220 pounds in a nanosecond?

"When we get home," he said to his

daughter, "we'll give you a bath and a bottle. We'll play, too."

More kicks and waves. Lots of vocalizing.

"She's really bonding with you, Dan. That part of the plan is working out perfectly."

"I hope so. She needs to be happy with me."

"And the kids were great with her, too. They all wanted to hold her, not to mention Theresa and Mary Ann almost fighting over her." Alexis rattled on so quickly, her words bumped into one another. "We're going to have one spoiled baby here."

Something was wrong. Her words were encouraging, but her tone was odd. He snapped on the reading light and looked at Alexis who was biting her bottom lip.

The barracuda was easy to read tonight. "Michelle needs you, too, Auntie. I know that. When the season's over, we're not letting you disappear."

"You can't," she said quickly. "I reminded Andy Romano about the visitation papers earlier."

Disappointed that she still didn't trust him, Dan said nothing.

"Andy said they were ready," she continued.

"I could have told you that," Dan said.

"But you didn't. When the season ends, or if

you get married again one day, Michelle needs to know she can count on me."

"I promise, you won't have to worry about that." He'd always maintained that Kim had been his one and only, and the pain of watching her lose the battle—the pain of losing her—had been too much. That's when he'd started to drink heavily. But he hadn't had a drink since…was it the day Alexis and Michelle had visited him that very first time? He thought about the days and weeks afterward. He was right. He hadn't touched the stuff since their first visit. Not that he hadn't had the urge. He had. So what did that mean? Was he merely enjoying a temporary reprieve, because of the distraction of Alexis and Michelle? Or was he in control of Jack Daniel's after all?

He played with the baby and studied the woman—both precious cargo. Fear sluiced through him as he wondered if, in the end, alcohol would put that precious cargo at risk. He needed to find out quickly.

Suddenly, Alexis smiled and gestured at the stadium, now in the distance. "If you keep your word about not remarrying, you're going to disappoint a lot of love-struck fans out there."

Glad she'd lightened the mood, he leaned

back, one arm going around her. His fingers automatically stroked her hair, the back of her neck.

"Oh, that feels good," she murmured, "but I think you deserve a massage more than I do after a three-hour game."

"Sixty minutes plus OT."

Alexis lifted her arm and tapped her watch. "Uh, what time is it?"

She had a point. Sixty minutes on the clock usually took three hours to play. "I love this side of you," he replied, taking her hand but ignoring the timepiece. "The funny, bantering Ally." He kissed her palm and felt her shiver.

"Strange, but I've never had a nickname before."

"Do you mind?" he asked. "Counselor Alexis Brown can knock 'em out in court, but I think Ally suits you more at home."

Her temporary home. "Ally's fine. In fact, I like it. And it will be easier for Michelle to say, anyway. But speaking of home—look at that traffic. Louis will have to double-park."

Dan scanned the scene out the window. They'd arrived on Chestnut Street, and Ally was right. There were no parking spots near his house at all, and several cars were already double-parked.

Louis's voice came through the speaker. "Mr. Delito, we definitely have a situation here."

"What does he mean?" asked Alexis. "What situation?"

"Paparazzi," Dan explained. "Louis and I have handled this before. Just do what I tell you."

He tamped down the anger that flared at the sight of the vultures with their cameras. Hadn't they done enough to make his life miserable two years ago? Getting mad never changed anything, he reminded himself. And he had to take the unpleasant trappings of his fame along with the good ones.

Dan unstrapped Michelle from her car seat and handed her to Alexis. "Get your house key out and in your hand. Louis will come around and get you with an umbrella that he'll open to prevent pictures. You take Michelle directly inside the house. At the same time, I'll exit the car on the street side and distract them."

Their limo came to a halt. Car doors slammed up and down the block. As Dan had predicted, Louis got out and walked to the trunk of their vehicle.

"As soon as Louis opens the umbrella and pulls open your door, you go!"

She nodded. "I understand."

They scrambled, and the choreography worked. A minute later, Dan, Ally and Michelle were inside the town house, Louis back in the car. No harm done, but Ally's complexion had paled.

"The lights! You didn't mention all those strobe lights. I think they got us after all. What if the baby's picture is in the paper? She'd be recognized, she could be kidnapped—"

Wanting to play it cool and calm her down, Dan shrugged. Yawned. Stretched his arms slowly over his head. "You've worked too many criminal cases. Relax. It's too late now. Whatever will be, will be."

"Whatever will…?" Alexis stared at him in disbelief. "That's very Zen of you, and totally *not* you at all. You took charge out on that street as though you were on the gridiron. I don't believe a word you're saying now. What's going on?"

She was sharp. He'd known from the beginning that he'd have a hard time staying one step ahead of her. But he had a plan—a good plan—to handle the paparazzi, and he didn't want her to worry. Oh, well, he'd always loved a challenge, and she was as tough as the Dolphins had been that day.

"Not believe me? Why, Ally, you're breaking my heart."

He was playing, teasing, trying to distract her. But rather than garnering a smile, his words seemed to puzzle his housemate. Her crinkled brow cleared for a moment, but only a moment, before the frown returned. She began biting her lip before lifting her hand and touching his cheek.

"Truth, Dan. I must have the truth," she said, her lips trembling. "You're acting crazy. I don't recognize you. Have you been drinking again?"

SLEEPING WAS OUT. In her room across the hall from the baby's, Alexis tossed and turned. She'd hurt him. She'd seen the shock, followed by a mask of indifference, after she'd asked her question. Then he'd taken the baby, changed her, fed her and put her to bed. The message had been loud and clear: nanny not required. She'd blown it, and her guilt surged further because Dan had really needed to soak in a hot tub, but he'd chosen to care for Michelle instead. He'd probably pay a price for that tomorrow.

Vodka left no odor. She knew that much. Vodka was one of her father's favorites for that very reason, so her suspicious nature had taken over. She knew nothing about what went on in the locker room after a winning game—except, of course, for all the sports drink that was poured on the coach sometimes. But maybe the guys tied one on. Or two. Dan had given her no real cause for suspicion. He'd been teasing, but she'd quickly jumped to the explanation that had always held up in the past when her parents had acted crazy. Alcohol. No wonder he was insulted.

She switched on the nightstand lamp and got out of bed. If he was still up, he'd get an apology now. She'd left her door ajar, the better to hear Michelle in the middle of the night. Now she pulled it the rest of the way open—and almost crashed into Dan, whose hand was poised to knock.

With his shaggy dark hair, luminous eyes and hooded lids, Dan looked like a man able to melt a woman's bones. Caught by the image, she was totally adrift. Totally in trouble.

"I'm sorry, Dan," she said, finally breaking the silence. "I should never have asked that."

"If you think it, you should ask. I like things out in the open, which is what I wanted to tell you. You can't feel comfortable living here if you're afraid of me."

"But I'm not afraid of you. I know my way around alcoholics and their enablers. Sherri and I had plenty of practice in survival. Reading expressions, tiptoeing around, making ourselves scarce. Once, we invested our little bits of money to buy locks for our bedroom door to keep Cal—my father—out."

"What?"

The horror in his voice had her shaking her

head. "He never caught her—I mean, us. Luckily, he was usually so drunk when he looked our way, he never made it up the stairs. But we weren't taking any chances." She paused, memories haunting her. "His fists, I remember—they were big, they were fast. He wanted to be a boxer, a professional, when he was a kid. We didn't always escape those fists."

She felt like crying, which was exactly the reason she didn't like getting involved too closely with people, why she didn't have a coterie of friends. Too much sharing. She didn't need to talk about this stuff.

Dan's gentle hands stroked her cheeks, arms, shoulders.

She wanted to lean against him, against his broad chest, but resisted.

He pulled her in.

"I'm not afraid of you," she repeated, this time mumbling into his shirt. "You're not like Cal at all. If total abstinence works for you, like this week, then I'm all for it."

"You know all the labels, and I know nothing."

With his finger beneath her chin, he tilted her head back and leaned down. He was going to kiss her. She knew it, wanted it, had been waiting for it.

Hold on, Brown. Yes, he's attractive—oh my,

yes. And yes he's sympathetic and warm. But you're an employee here, and he may well be a drunk. And don't forget, he's spent the past two years casually hooking up with women to forget his dead wife. Use your head.

With the sort of determination that had seen her through childhood, through law school, through Sherri's death, Alexis forced herself to pull away from him. His eyes widened, but he immediately stepped back. He cleared his throat.

"Well, um, yeah," he mumbled. "It's getting late. I should let you get some sleep."

Her heart crumbled at the look on his face, but she stood firm. The deal when she'd agreed to work here was that there would be no romantic involvements. It was the only practical choice.

"Yes, Michelle will have me up early. Gotta get my beauty rest." She forced a lightness she didn't feel into her voice. "Goodnight."

Without looking back, she walked into her bedroom and closed the door. Only when she heard Dan's footsteps moving down the hallway did she allow herself to collapse against the wood and fantasize, just a little, about what might have been if they both hadn't been so damned sensible.

CHAPTER EIGHT

FOLLOWING DAN'S SUGGESTIONS, Alexis stayed close to home for the next few days. She finally appreciated Maria's system of calling in food orders and having deliveries made. Michelle napped on the back patio, getting her fresh air, while Alexis sat with her, reading child-care manuals and highlighting items to discuss with Dan. In her view, however, she was living in a comfortable prison.

By Tuesday, the photographers seemed to have disappeared. By Wednesday, she was bursting to be free, and when Dan called to say he'd be late that evening and every Wednesday thereafter, because he had to go to a meeting, she made up her mind to take a walk with Michelle. The day was chilly, but sunny blue skies beckoned. In early November, winter approached quickly. There would be snow in a few weeks.

Caring for Michelle was like playing with a live doll, thought Alexis, as she dressed the baby for the weather. Michelle looked adorable in her pink-and-white snowsuit and knit hat with two pom-poms on top. Alexis attached the wind cover to the appropriate hooks on the stroller, stepped outside and glanced up and down the street.

All seemed quiet. No double-parked cars. No one loitered, so she took a deep refreshing breath and started off at her usual brisk pace.

In five minutes, her memories kicked in, reminding her of the days when she and Michelle lived alone, anonymously, and long walks through the city were part of their daily routine. A month seemed like a lifetime ago. Contacting Dan Delito had changed everything.

She reached Charles Street and slowed down to browse the windows of its many antique and gift shops, something she'd never had time to do when she worked in the D.A.'s office. Although she knew nothing about them, the antiques captured her imagination. Similar items were displayed in Dan's house.

An hour later, she entered one of the lovely restaurants in the neighborhood, ready for a cup of tea and a place to feed and change the baby.

The venue was crowded, and she had to maneuver the stroller to a table near the back. After removing Michelle's outerwear and her own jacket, she finally sat down.

The waitress appeared, took her order, then tapped her pencil on her pad. "You look familiar, but I don't remember you coming in here before."

Alexis shrugged. "I seem to have one of those common faces. Everyone thinks they know me."

The waitress smiled. "Maybe so." She shrugged. "I must be getting old, imagining things. I'll be right back with the tea and sandwich."

"And I'll be changing the baby in the ladies' room."

Her food was just being served when Alexis returned.

"Here's your order, honey. Plus something extra. No charge." The woman placed a newspaper on the table. "Thought I recognized you from somewhere," she said before disappearing to assist other customers.

It wasn't a newspaper, but an entertainment tabloid. On the front page, a large close-up of herself stared back at Alexis. A younger version—a college photo. The slant of the story made her feel sick:

ALEXIS BROWN REPLACES DEAD SISTER

Hometown hero Dan Delito likes the Brown sisters so much, he fathered a baby girl with one and keeps the other locked away to care for her. Will the new baby soon have a sister of her own?

The story continued, citing reliable sources of information, including an "official" interview with a certain Calvin Brown. Lies and more lies. Especially stunning when the man somehow connected Sherri's "despair over Dan's rejection" with her death.

Alexis froze, too stunned at the moment to feel the disgust for Cal, the disappointment that always simmered somewhere inside her. Ever the manipulator, ever eager to make an easy buck, her father would make sure he got paid well for his mishmash of fact and fiction. This was exactly the type of story the tabloids loved, and to hell with the truth. Cal had a copy of the police report. He'd gotten the facts but had conveniently forgotten them.

What to do? She had to get out of the restaurant. Then she'd think about suing the paper for libel. Or she could decide to ignore the article. She'd speak to Dan before making a decision.

Reaching into her wallet to throw a few bills on the table, she began to pack up. But the baby was fussy and had to be fed. Taking a quick glance around the room, Alexis was relieved to note that everyone was busy with their own meals and conversations. She reached for the infant, sat back down and offered the bottle. Ever-greedy Michelle latched on and sighed.

Tears welled in Alexis's eyes. "I love you more than you can know, sweetheart. I promise to take good care of you."

Ten minutes later, she was ready to walk out the restaurant door. But when she opened it, the plethora of strobe lights blinded her, shocking her like an act of terrorism on a personal level.

She stepped back inside and reached for her cell phone. Not to call Dan. She'd never interrupt a practice session, not when the entire world was watching every move the quarterback made. Not when millions and millions of dollars rested on him and his team. And besides, his appearance would be more food for the bottom-feeders.

She punched in the number of the Sudbury Street police station, the closest station to Dan's house. With just a little help from her colleagues, Alexis Brown could take care of herself.

"YOU CALLED THE COPS instead of calling me?" Dan's voice hit a high note of disbelief.

Whoops. Had she made a mistake? His incredulous expression said she had, but at nine o'clock that night, she was too tired to cater to his ego, too frustrated to be polite. They hadn't even discussed a possible lawsuit yet, which, of course, wouldn't help right now. Would she ever be able to leave the house safely?

"And what could you have done except add to the chaos on a public sidewalk? I've got a lot of friends among Boston's finest in station houses all over the city. Where do you think I got cases to prosecute?"

But he wasn't listening. In the second-floor game room, Alexis watched Dan pace. "You could have called Louis," he said. "He would have known what to do."

She inclined her head. "Possibly, but I didn't think of him right then. I've worked with Sergeant Polikoff in the past, and he knew exactly how to handle the situation. He covered us with blankets and whisked us into his patrol car without an inch of our skin showing. He threw the stroller in the trunk. He was great."

His eyes narrowed. "So I'll send him two tickets to the next home game," he snapped. "Will that make you happy?"

"Happy? What's that got to do with any-thing?" She walked toward him with deliberate steps. "What's gotten into you?" she asked, stabbing his chest with her index finger. "Michelle escaped pictures—" stab "—so did I." Another stab. "Which was the whole point. What's wrong?"

And then she couldn't speak. He captured her hand with his larger one, and his mouth covered hers in a kiss that sent a shock wave through her entire body. She responded to him immediately with equal fervor. His lips were hard on hers, hungry, devouring. He wrapped her in his arms, pulled her tightly against him. He was hard between her thighs, too, but she remained close, unafraid.

This wasn't about lovemaking, or about sexual intimacy. This was about his fear and need for reassurance.

"Nothing's wrong now," he said, bestowing soft kisses on her neck, around her ear. "You're safe, the baby's safe. Just remember one thing, Ally."

She tipped her head back to see him better, his dark-as-midnight eyes capturing her. "What?" she whispered.

"I take care of my own," he said. "Always

have, always will. So next time there's a problem, sweetheart, you call me."

She swallowed hard. That philosophy wouldn't work for her, and he wouldn't understand. Stroking his face, she softly said, "Danny, I'm not your Kim. I'm healthy and strong. I can take care of myself. Always have, always will."

He didn't blink, just kept his arm around her. "You missed the point. It's not about health or stamina. You're living under my roof, you're family and I'm responsible. End of story."

Alexis knew any other woman would have swooned at the prospect of such safety and protection. But she was not any other woman.

"That's not the way it works, Dan, at least not for me. I've virtually been on my own since I was fourteen. I can navigate pretty well. You are off the hook."

She looked past his shoulder, eyes unfocused, not seeing anything but memories, scenes she rarely thought about anymore. "When I was a kid, I dreamed of running away and finding different parents for Sherri and me. Cal drank so much, and he was a real mean drunk. The place was a mess. My mother was useless. Sherri was so little and confused, and I promised to take care of her. But in the end, I didn't, and she died." Unprepared for the grief that slammed into her, she cradled her cramping stomach, her usual reaction to stress.

"You helped save her child!" Dan protested. "Saving Michelle was the best gift of all. You *are* keeping your promise to Sherri."

His arms swaddled her now, and she felt kisses on her temple, as soothing and sweet as his words. She leaned into him, allowing herself to feel safe, allowing herself to depend on someone else—for a moment. Then she stepped back.

"The man who killed her was an old boyfriend—that part was in the newspaper article. We found out later that the guy had just been released from prison. He thought Sherri would be waiting for him. When he saw she was pregnant, he went ballistic."

He emitted his familiar low whistle. "The cops told you?"

She nodded. "A while ago. I have a copy of their investigation."

"Why didn't you tell me?"

Surprised at the question, she didn't respond for a moment. She never shared personal problems with anyone, and she hadn't volunteered this information, either, not even to Roz. Maybe she should have.

"You didn't need to know," she finally

replied. "It's not your burden to bear. It's mine. You have your own demons."

"I'm working on those," he said, "seriously working on them. But I could have helped you, Ally. We're a team. We're very good friends. And that's what friends do."

Did "friends" kiss they way they just had? She decided not to ask. Instead, she said, "Telling you wouldn't have changed the outcome. You couldn't undo the crime."

"Oh, baby. You don't get it." He reached for her again, rocked her where they stood, her entire body touching his. "It's not about the crime. It's about the aftermath."

"I'm used to stomachaches afterward."

"Tell me more about what happened."

"All right," she said, holding on to his hand. She began speaking slowly, each word an effort.

"The perp had ID on him. They questioned his cell mates, his landlord, his parole officer—the works. That's how they put the whole thing together. My sister was simply looking for love—" she gulped "—in all the wrong places."

"I'm so sorry, Ally. So very sorry about Sherri. But I know she would be happy you're here with us. You're the best mother Michelle could have."

She didn't want to think anymore. Or talk

anymore. She just wanted his arms around her again. "Could you just, uh, hold me for a little bit longer?"

In an instant, she was tucked against him, her head on his broad chest. She heard his heart pounding in a strong, steady beat under her ear. At this moment, she needed someone strong and steady by her side. But she knew it couldn't last. When they'd promised to keep their relationship professional, they'd made the right choice.

That didn't mean she couldn't take strength from his comfort for a few minutes more, though.

"Thanks, Danny," she said, wrapping her arms around his waist. "You're a good listener."

"I told you, Ally," he said in a voice as warm and smooth as caramel, "I always take care of my own."

"Even a temporary nanny?" She laughed, trying to keep things light as she reminded him that he was her employer and that she wouldn't be living here forever.

"Definitely. Especially the independent types."

Alexis cleared her throat. She didn't want to say it, but it had to be said. "You know this can't happen again, right?"

"What?" he asked, all innocence but with a gleam in his eye.

"This." She nodded to their entwined bodies

even as she pulled away from him. "We agreed when I got here that we'd keep things professional. I don't think either one of us is ready for a relationship." Especially the man with the weakness for beer and a heart that belongs to his dead wife.

"I did promise, and I'm a man of my word." He retreated a step and sighed. "Geez, it's hard having integrity sometimes."

She smiled even as she yearned to return to the warmth of his arms. "Tell me about it."

MARIA HAD ALREADY ARRIVED when Dan entered the kitchen the next morning. Without a word, she laid yesterday's fiasco on the table, and Dan realized for the first time that he'd never actually seen the story in print. His blood pressure spiked as he read. What smut. What salacious reporting. He'd help Ally sue their asses off.

He waited until Alexis and Michelle had made their appearance and greeted Maria before picking up the phone. He glanced at Ally. "I figured out how to put the tabloids to rest, and I want you to listen in. I'm putting the call on speaker."

"Great. I'm open to any idea that guarantees me freedom and safety."

He punched in Sean Callan's number.

"We've got a situation here, Coach, that needs to be handled ASAP—and, by the way, you're on speaker."

"We know all about it. Yesterday's rag circulated among management all day."

"Well, I have an idea," Dan said.

"So do we."

"A press conference," Dan continued. "All the legitimate stringers for major papers and all the national outlets—Associated Press, Reuters, you name it."

"Exactly," said Sean. "Beat 'em at their own game. I'll tell Rick you're on board. And he'll get to top management."

"Wait a minute," Alexis called out. "Who's Rick? And why a press conference? I thought we didn't like the press. And aren't you worried about Michelle's picture being in the paper?"

"Nope," said Dan, walking to the pantry, the phone connection still active. "I'd be much more worried if the paparazzi kept hiding out on the street. This way, they'll be scooped by legit papers, and they'll go hassle someone else."

"Rick Thompson's the head coach," Dan continued. "I thought I wrote all these numbers down for you at the beginning."

She shrugged, then turned in a slow circle,

finally pointing at the side of the fridge. "There they are."

But Dan knew she'd never consider calling any of his people. Not Ms. Independence.

"So, Ms. Brown," came Sean Callan's voice. "Are you on board with this?"

She hesitated. "I suppose, as long as my picture isn't taken."

"Can't promise. But we'll focus on Dan and the baby. The point is to spin the headline from you and your sister to a Dan the Daddy kind of thing."

The call ended with Sean promising to have the details worked out by the time Dan got to the stadium that day. Alexis felt breathless.

"Boy, when you fellows make a decision, you follow through at the speed of light."

Dan shrugged. "Maybe it's a guy thing."

"Nope," replied Ally, handing the baby to her father. "I think it's a Dan thing. And maybe a goal thing. You're always talking about goals."

His eyes brightened. "They keep life interesting." And then he leaned over and kissed her. "Fair warning."

Maria beamed. "Now we have a good story, no?"

"Oh, absolutely," said Dan, pulling up his chair and reaching for his cereal. "A very good story, if the main character cooperates."

HER LIFE WAS NOT FICTION, however, and real-life people didn't fall into place like characters in a book. Sure, she had warm feelings for Dan. He was a great guy. Sensitive, kind, a wonderful father and up-front about learning everything he could about babies. She admired him for asking questions. Their relationship was geared to Michelle, the way it was supposed to be. And he hadn't touched a drop of liquor in—well, she didn't quite know in how long, but at least not since she'd been living with him.

With few exceptions, they almost always focused on the baby. Last Wednesday night had been a definite exception. He'd held her, comforted her and kissed her.

Now, it was almost noon the following Monday, and she was waiting for Louis to bring him home from the airport after yesterday's game in Buffalo. Another win for New England, but she knew better than to offer too many kudos. Athletes seemed to be a very superstitious bunch. Rita, Nicky, and Joe, and their kids hadn't held back their cheers, however, when they'd watched the Buffalo game with her and Michelle. She'd assumed Dan's house was the usual family gathering place.

"Oh, no, Ally," Rita had said when Alexis

had mentioned it. "You'll all be coming to my house after this—this—tabloid business is over. Grandma and Grandpa love to host the away games. We love everyone being together with us. And Thanksgiving is coming up, too."

The "tabloid business" would be handled the next day at the press conference at Gillette Stadium. Over the weekend, however, there'd been a follow-up story, just as salacious as the first. Cal had found true kinship with the paparazzi, at both his daughters' expense, and had manipulated Peggy to offer a quote.

If Alexis hadn't known his M.O. so well, she would have puked. At this point, she laughed. Cal would never change because he didn't want to. Peggy took care of him, and he was happy. Alexis had figured all that out when she was fourteen and hadn't changed her mind. They were not her problem anymore.

A jingle of keys at the door distracted her. Instantly, her heartbeat quickened with excitement. Carrying the baby, she walked toward the front of the house.

Dan filled the doorway with his physical presence and filled the air with his energy. In two long strides, he was with them, a kiss for the baby and a quick hug for her, his arms going around them both.

"How are my girls?" he asked, while taking an excited Michelle and covering her with kisses. Without waiting for a response, he added, "I love coming home now."

And I love seeing him walk through that door.

I love the light in his eyes when he looks my way.

I love fitting so well against him when he holds me.

And his kisses last night were incredible.

But does he see Ally or Kim's angel?

Is he an alcoholic?

I'm a temporary nanny helping him out of a tight spot.

And I am in big trouble.

Alexis could see his happiness, feel his happiness. He was definitely a family man. No wonder the last few years had been a living hell for him. Well, that wasn't her problem, either.

"It's funny how you love coming home to a crowd, and I've always enjoyed living alone," she said. "I never questioned it, never yearned for anything else. I guess I like my space. I like to focus on my own goals and enjoy my successes."

His head whipped around. "But who do you

share them with? Sometimes a person's priorities shift, Ally. Take it from an expert."

THE NEXT MORNING, ALEXIS found herself back at Gillette Stadium. The press corps was there in full measure. Reporters from newspapers and magazines, regional and national, all with badges to prove their credentials, crowded into a big meeting room.

"Time for the dog and pony show," Dan whispered to her after the team's PR person introduced him and laid out the process for the occasion. Dan would make a statement, show the baby, answer a few questions.

He stepped to the microphone with Michelle while Alexis remained in the background.

"I'd like you all to meet my daughter, Michelle Brown Delito. She's four months old and the best gift a man could receive. Sometimes, a surprise works out absolutely perfectly."

He paused, and Alexis nodded to herself. Clever timing, to buy a moment for the idea to sink into their consciousness.

"As you know," he continued, "Michelle's mother, Sherri Brown, is deceased. She is sorrowfully missed by all of us. But with my family's help—and there are a lot of us—and the help of Michelle's devoted aunt, Alexis

Brown, my daughter will have plenty of women in her life, women who love her very much."

He surveyed the crowd and invited their questions.

"So, are you going from Dapper Dan to Diaper Dan?"

Everyone laughed and Dan grinned. "I sure am. I've learned a lot about babies in the last month and can change a diaper pretty well now."

"How will the baby affect your career? Are you going to retire earlier than planned?"

"Retire? Hell, no! I'll be playing longer. My folks tell me kids cost money. A lot of money. So, hopefully, I'll be working for years to come."

So far, so good, thought Ally. Dan really knew how to handle reporters' questions, from serious types to lighthearted ones.

"New England's hot, Dan. The team's hot. Three times before you've taken us to the Super Bowl and we've won twice. What about this year?"

"No comment." His mouth tightened, his brows contracted. He shook his head.

And Alexis jumped forward. "Dan concentrates on one game at a time. The team does, as well. You should know that by now," she scolded. *Two Super Bowl wins? Man, I need to look the guy up on Google.*

Snap, snap, snap. Cameras clicked and flashed. Dan's eyes gleamed with delight. Now his smile grew and he pulled her against him.

"How's that for a defense? Meet my new coach," he said. "Thanks to Alexis, I've learned how to take care of Michelle."

"I have a question for Ms. Brown," said a reporter. "You're now living with Dan in his home, teaching him how to care for the baby. So, is that the only relationship between the two of you, or can we expect a different kind of announcement in the future?"

She felt Dan stiffen beside her and squeezed his arm.

Stepping to the mike, she said, "It's really simple. You just heard the man say it, and you said it yourself. I'm the daddy coach. Dan and I both love Michelle. We believe the more people who love a child, the better off that child is. Now Michelle has two of us—two people whom she recognizes and loves. Two people who'd go to hell and back for her."

"Well said, Alexis." Dan took over, and Alexis stepped out of camera range again. "Dan," called a voice from the back. "I want to check out some of the claims floating around. What, exactly, was your relationship with Sherri Brown?"

Alexis felt her stomach pinch, but forced herself to remain calm. Debunking Cal's outrageous statements was the reason for the press conference.

Dan took a breath. Alexis knew the team's PR rep had coached him on ways to respond to this inevitable question, but she knew it wouldn't be easy.

"Sherri was a fan," he began in a warm, steady voice. "I know I don't need to tell you that fans and players sometimes strike up relationships. Not all of them are lasting ones. Neither of us was seeking anything long term when we met. We enjoyed each other's company, but we soon moved on. We weren't as careful as we could have been, and Michelle is the delightful result."

Alexis relaxed slightly. Dan had put a positive spin on the situation. It was going to be all right.

"Mr. Delito, when did you find out Sherri Brown had been murdered?" barked a brittle-looking woman in the front row.

The question struck Alexis like a punch in the gut. Even now, the words *Sherri* and *murdered* sounded obscene in the same sentence.

Dan, however, maintained the same calm voice. "I found out last month, from her sister,

Alexis, at the same time I learned of Michelle's existence."

"Why didn't Sherri tell you about the baby?"

Alexis closed her eyes. The questions felt like a volley of bullets.

"I can't pretend to read Sherri's mind. She had her own reasons, which she didn't even share with her sister. Alexis learned I was the father the night Sherri died."

Uh-oh. That might have been Dan's first misstep. Alexis, so used to observing lawyers cross-examine witnesses, heard the next question in her head before it was even asked.

"So why did Alexis Brown wait three months to tell you?" the brittle woman asked.

Dan shot Alexis a warning look. *Don't rise to the bait,* his eyes told her. *Let me handle this.*

She clamped her fingers around the edge of her seat to keep from flying out of it. It was almost impossible to stay quiet while he spoke for her, but she knew he was right. This was his show.

"Alexis was grieving her sister's death," he said slowly. "She was also dealing with police, courts and wills, as well and trying to care for a newborn. She didn't exactly have a lot of spare time or energy on her hands."

A gentle chuckle echoed through the room. Trust Dan to defuse the tension.

"Also, she had never met me. She didn't know anything about me. Amazingly she'd never even seen a Patriots game."

More laughter.

"What she did know was that Sherri had asked her to keep Michelle safe. And until she had the time and resources to find out a bit more about me, she wanted to be careful about revealing Michelle's existence. Completely prudent, wouldn't you say?"

Alexis noticed a couple of reporters nodding. She suppressed a small grin. He hadn't been quite so sanguine about her secrecy when he'd first learned of it. But he was doing an excellent job now of pretending he had been.

He fielded a few more innocuous questions before saying, "We appreciate your support, ladies and gentlemen. You can always count on me for an interview concerning the team. Ms. Brown and I, and Michelle, too, appreciate your professionalism. Thanks for coming today. Now you may take as many pictures of Michelle and me as you'd like. In fact, take some great shots so the paparazzi won't continue to stalk the ladies."

Alexis heard murmurs of "class act" and "cute kid," and "Dan, hold the baby up higher." Dan complied. The photographers were focused on father and child, just as they should be. She heard Michelle gurgle her baby talk. The reporters now had a full story and could write their articles based on today's discussion. Dan and the team's management had accomplished their goals.

Satisfied and encouraged, Alexis was ready to put the paparazzi experiences behind her. She glanced at father and child just as Michelle lifted her head from Dan's shoulder and spotted her. Immediately, the infant reached out and babbled. She squirmed, squealed and almost jumped from Dan's arms. Then she started to cry.

Dan motioned Ally closer. In a moment, she stood next to him, holding a happy Michelle. Cameras flashed again, and Alexis understood that this time the pictures would include the three of them together.

Little Michelle had managed to make a statement of her own.

CHAPTER NINE

NINE DAYS LATER, ON Thanksgiving morning, the entire kitchen counter was covered with vegetables—fresh vegetables, canned vegetables— more produce than Dan had ever seen at any one time in any kitchen except at his family's store. Ally stood in front of the sink, looking left, then right, then totally lost. Michelle was pounding on a toy on her play mat.

Standing in the doorway, hands high up against the frame, Dan said, "So, what's going on?"

Ally threw him a halfhearted smile. "I volunteered to toss a salad. We can't show up at your mother's empty-handed, and I figured even I could throw a little salad together."

"Little? Did you say little? You'll need at least five bowls for all that stuff."

She glared at him. "Maria bought a lot."

"Oh, I get it. It's the old 'blame Maria' story," he teased, and then joined in when Alexis broke out laughing.

She sounded so free, so lighthearted, and looked so scrumptious, he couldn't resist. In the midst of their silliness, he kissed her.

He could swear electricity crackled between them. He'd felt the spark when his mouth touched hers and she parted her lips, welcoming him in. So, he went further, tasting, touching, his tongue meeting hers in a getting-to-know-you-dance, and a wanting-to-know-you-better encore.

He held her, pulled her close and just breathed her in. His hands roved, stroking her shoulder, her side, then across her back, and lower, just above her bottom. He followed her waist and came around front, his thumb finding its way across her breast. He heard her gasp, then moan softly...and loved the sound. Brushing his finger across her nipple again, he felt it harden, heard the moan rev up a notch, this time with his name attached. And had to force himself to hold still.

Talk about hard. He was standing at stiff attention and was afraid he'd scare her off.

"Dan, Danny..." She kissed him again and seemed oblivious to his situation.

"Easy, baby, easy," he soothed.

"What?" She shook her head, took a step back. He watched her breathe.

Full of confusion, those moss-green eyes appealed to him. "What are we doing?" she whispered. "This can't be good."

Her statements brought him up short. She was right. As wonderful as kissing her felt, it wasn't a smart idea. They'd just finished telling a roomful of reporters that they had a strictly business relationship. And he'd promised her he wouldn't take advantage of her presence in his house. He had to try to be a man of his word.

He also had to make sure he was the man she deserved. Less than two months ago, he'd been drinking away his grief over Kim's death. Was he truly over Kim? And was he truly free of the bottle?

Even though every muscle he possessed screamed out to touch Alexis again, he ignored the sensation. He was used to telling his body what to do. And until he knew the answers to those questions, he'd try to keep his relationship with Alexis friendly and warm, but not romantic. It was only fair to her.

Turning around and crossing the kitchen, he reached into an upper cabinet, pulled out two extra-large round trays and put one on each side of the sink. "So how'd you like to learn something new?" he asked, keeping his voice light.

"I'm going to teach you how to make an Italian antipasto."

"Sure! Just let me get a notebook so I can write everything down."

He groaned. Loudly. Took her hands, and then thought better of it and dropped them.

"It's not rocket science. Just follow what I do."

"Okay, I will." She laughed, a little shakily. "See, Danny. I'm following, and I'm going with the flow."

He loved her playfulness.

He loved her courage.

But he had to back off. At least for now.

"BRACE YOURSELF," SAID DAN several hours later. "There's probably forty or fifty people in there. My folks keep adding to the guest list every year."

As Dan pulled into his parents' driveway, Alexis wondered how long they'd have to stay. At least an hour, she figured, maybe two, before they could politely make their getaway.

"It's a good thing we made two antipasto plates, then," she said.

"I had a lot of fun."

"It's always fun to make a big mess. But they look good, don't they? Even mine." She'd learned the craft of building a salad layer by layer, turning it into a work of art by not only using regular produce but also by adding cheeses, meats and fruits—like melon chunks wrapped in prosciutto—along with mounds of black and green olives in the middle. Dan had called it, "a feast for the eye and the stomach."

"I have a confession to make," she said as they walked to Rita and Nicky's front door, Michelle in her arms while Dan carried one of the salads.

"Sounds serious."

She sighed. "After we finished the antipastos, I sneaked upstairs and wrote it all down."

The front door opened just as Dan's gleeful laugh rang out.

"Now, that's the way to start a party!" said Nick, taking the baby. "Come on in."

"I'll get the other tray," said Alexis.

"Do that," said Dan, eyes glistening. "Then figure out what you'll do if we use different ingredients next time."

Alexis paused. "You're kidding, right?"

But Dan didn't answer. He just kept shaking his head as he watched her retrieve the second platter from the car.

At one o'clock, the house was already filled with people, but somehow, groups had formed. Women in the kitchen, kids in the family room, men in the living room. Nick still had the baby and Michelle seemed to be doing fine.

"These salads are beautiful!" said Rita, directing their placement at each end of the dining room table. "I didn't expect you to go to so much trouble."

"Dan helped," said Alexis quickly. "He helped a lot. And besides, look at all the work you've been doing."

"Ahem," snorted Theresa. "My mom has the fine art of delegating down to a science. We all brought side dishes and desserts, and yesterday we were here setting the table."

Despite Theresa's mock complaints, Alexis could feel the warmth and friendship among the women. Mary Ann, too, was at the stove, stirring something while throwing her comments into the conversation. To her great surprise, Alexis felt relaxed, almost as if she were part of the group.

"I guess this is how a holiday is supposed to feel," she said, "everyone helping and happy together."

"Or noisy and complaining," joked Rita, glancing at her daughter. "But, we all look forward to it. It's good family time."

"Lucky family." She heard the wistful note in her voice as she remembered all the Thanksgivings she and Sherri had stayed away from the house, away from Cal. The man didn't work on holidays, and they'd found other places to go, like public parks and second-run movie theaters.

"We've been especially lucky since you came around," said Rita.

Alexis smiled. "Babies are miracles, aren't they?"

"A loving and caring aunt is a miracle, too," said Theresa. "In fact, a couple of little girls I know think Michelle's auntie is an angel."

"She's *definitely* an angel." Dan joined them with Michelle in his arms. "She puts up with me and my crazy schedule and still keeps her sanity."

Placing Michelle in her lap, Dan leaned over her chair. He looked as though he was going to kiss her. She knew it. She could read his intention, his body language. "I don't think—"

What would his family think of her when Dan finished the football season, decided he no longer needed her nanny services and moved on? He'd already shown—with Sherri and who knew how many others—that he was quite willing to love 'em and leave 'em. Would the Delitos think she was just a good-time girl? Would they assume it ran in the family? Alexis felt sick.

Dan straightened. "See you later," he said. "After Joe, Dad and I throw the ball a few times."

"You need to go easy on your father," said Rita. "He's not twenty-one anymore."

"Could've fooled me," said Dan with a wink.

After he left the kitchen, Rita lowered herself into a chair and started to cry.

"Mom!" Theresa kneeled next to the woman. "It's okay. He'll be careful with Daddy. Don't worry."

But Rita shook her head. "I'm not worried about Dad. Don't you see what I see? It's Danny. He's alive again. Looking wonderful. I think we've finally got our Danny-boy back."

Alexis slipped out of the room. Although she also rejoiced in the changes they'd all seen in Dan, she certainly didn't want to hear their analysis of those changes. Her name might be mentioned more often than Michelle's, and that would not do. It would not do at all.

THIRTY MINUTES LATER, what had started as casual exercise had turned into a full-fledged practice session in the middle of the street. As Alexis watched from the front porch, men and boys of every age surrounded the quarterback, all wanting to be part of the action. Dan paid attention to everyone, dividing players into teams. Soon, jackets started coming off.

Little by little, Rita and Nicky's friends came

over to meet Michelle, and Alexis found herself in the midst of more people in one day than she normally did in a week. Her plans to slip out after an hour or two disappeared. Thanksgiving was an all-day party. Once again, she'd have to go with the flow.

As Alexis continued to watch the football activity, the men stepped aside, and Dan turned into a coach for the youngsters in the group.

"He looks like he's really enjoying himself," she said. "I didn't know he liked to coach."

"This is how Dan grew up," said Theresa, who had joined her on the porch. "Every day, he'd be out here with a passel of boys throwing a football. He majored in history when he went to college, though, in case he wanted to teach high school someday…after his big career."

His sister shrugged. "Almost every little boy dreams of becoming a professional athlete. Who knew his dream would come true?"

Dan had known. He'd made it happen. Alexis understood that part of him because they both had the tenacity of a bulldog.

Later, after she'd returned to the house and fed and changed Michelle, Dan came into the kitchen. His energy was high, his face flushed from the cold, and his smile… Well, when he smiled at her, she felt the heat.

"That was more fun than the game against Washington's going to be on Sunday." He opened the fridge and grabbed a can of cola. "I'm thirsty." He started gulping. "Where's Joe and Larry?"

"On the back porch, I think."

She watched him go to the door and look through the pane. He made no move to join the men.

"Something wrong, Dan?"

"Nope. I just see a couple of jackasses sharing a few beers—outdoors—like it was summer." He stepped onto the porch.

She went to the window and groaned. A six-pack. She slipped her jacket on and followed Dan. No pretense of politeness here. Anything to do with alcohol was her business. If Dan resented her, too bad.

"Why are you guys drinking cold beer outside in the cold weather?" asked Dan. "Come on in."

Joe looked up. Took his time. "The truth?"

"I'm guessing I already know."

"We didn't want to tempt you. So we decided to hide out back here," said Dan's brother.

"Hide out! Well, aren't you considerate? And here I thought I was an adult." His hands fisted as sarcasm laced his voice. "Yes, sir. The all-powerful Dan Delito can sure spoil Thanksgiving for his family. Now, get inside. I promise you I'm not tempted by any of it. Not beer, not Scotch, not anything."

Joe stood. "I'm not going anywhere yet. Just answer this question."

Alexis had barely breathed since Dan confronted the men. Now she held her breath entirely and listened.

"When did you have your last drink?" asked Joe.

"October 8." He glanced toward Alexis. "It was the day Alexis and Michelle came to the house the first time. I was blitzed."

"That's got to be at least six weeks," said Larry. "Not bad."

"You were blitzed, you say?" repeated Joe. "So, now I want to know why the hell she ever went back for a second visit."

Alexis gasped and stepped forward. "I'm glad you love your brother, Joe, but my decisions and my actions are my business and Dan's—not yours."

"Don't start going all high-and-mighty on me," Joe replied. "I'm the one who promised not to give up on him. My dad and I both promised. We'll be here for him if he needs us, no matter what, no matter where, no matter when."

And she wouldn't. That was the challenge he laid down, what he implied. "And that's terrific," said Alexis. "He'll have several fine people in his corner, which can only be a good thing."

She kept her gaze firmly on Joe and started her courtroom pace. "As the daughter of an alcoholic," she continued, "I am first and foremost in *Michelle's* corner. Now, you can go chew on that for a while."

"I'm calling it a draw," said Dan. "So, you all can listen to me and listen hard. I'm a big boy, and I'm taking care of myself. Have as many beers as you want, bro. I'm fine."

Joe's interference really didn't bother Alexis. She hoped, however, that Dan had told the truth—that he'd been facing his problem, a problem that affected everyone around him. No amount of nagging or begging on her part could make him change—sobriety had to be his choice. Even her own father had gone through periods of sobriety along the way. Unfortunately, they'd never lasted for more than a few weeks. As for Dan—he might be going down the same path. The mere thought made her wince, made her stomach cramp. Worst of all, it made her heart ache.

Despite how wary she'd been when they'd first met, she was no match for a family man with a sense of humor. A man who tried hard to do the right thing, in good times and bad. A man who thought his daughter hung the moon, that every squeak and squawk, every new accomplishment of hers, was a miracle. Which, of course, it was.

As ironic as it seemed, Alexis had allowed Dan Delito to steal his way into her heart. *Ironic* was too mild a word to describe the situation, a situation that was reinforced by her periods of daydreaming. Alexis had never indulged in daydreams before. She'd been too practical for that. Now, she could barely recognize herself when she drifted off.

But daydreams weren't reality. Alexis had learned that years ago by watching her own mother, who obviously saw something in Cal Brown the rest of the world didn't. Perhaps Alexis's daydream image of Dan—a big man with gentle hands, who knew how to love— was accurate. But perhaps she was simply seeing what she wanted and he really was drowning his grief in hidden bottles of vodka. Until she was sure, she had to be careful. For her sake and Michelle's.

IT WAS ALMOST A RELIEF when Dan went out of town the next weekend. His Wednesdays away from home helped, too. He'd never told her exactly where he went on those nights, but he had referred to his activities as meetings.

She'd conjured up a number of possibilities—a team meeting at the stadium, or a dinner out with his players or even an AA meeting. Only one other option worried her. The "happy hours" constantly promoted by clubs and restaurants in the city. These social times were a magnet for young singles, and even she had gone once or twice with coworkers. Dan would fit in well if he was still looking to bury the pain of losing Kim. He could have stretched the definition of "meeting" easily enough. In her experience, alcoholics lied more easily and more often than they spoke the truth.

One day, she'd come right out and ask him where he went. So far, she had no cause to question him. He came home sober and smiling, happy to see her. Which was why she needed more of her own space.

Every time she saw him, she wanted him. And he knew it. He'd flirt with her, hug her, murmur in her ear. But he kept his word, the promise he'd made to her before she came to live with him and Michelle. He was respecting her boundaries. Definitely a good idea, but sometimes—despite her best efforts—she wanted what she was missing.

Impatient with herself now, she tried to focus on the computer screen. She needed to get her head together, to figure out what to do besides daydream about the man. On this last Friday night in November, she was browsing the Internet for possible job leads, a definite back-to-reality exercise. Not that it distracted her from anticipating Dan's phone call. Whenever he traveled, he called from his host city, and tonight he'd be in New York, ready to face the Jets on Sunday. Hopefully, the Patriots would add to their wins, as they'd done last week against the Redskins.

She chuckled, thinking about Dan's unwillingness to admit that with their 12–1 record so far, they were having a remarkable season. She went along with him and never, ever mentioned the *S* word. She was certain, however, that all of Boston was speculating.

When her cell rang, she answered immediately and heard, "Hi, Ally."

"Hi, yourself. So, you've arrived safe and sound?"

"Yep, except for one omission. No wallet. So, before I cancel credit cards, will you check my bedroom? And maybe the game room?"

"Sure. I'm walking toward your bedroom now and…let's just say it's pretty messy."

"Sorry. I left in a rush."

"Good excuse. But I don't want to pry. So where should I look?"

She followed his directions—a quick search of his night table drawer and the floor under the bed, the bathroom counter, the top of his dresser. No wallet anywhere.

"I'm going to need more time to be thorough. How about if I call you back?"

After he agreed, she disconnected the call and began searching more slowly, starting in the bathroom where he'd showered right before Louis had picked him up to go to the airport. A balled-up undershirt lay on the floor, but no wallet beneath. The vanity was pretty clear except for a lovely ceramic dish with some coins but no wallet. She opened the top drawer on the off chance the wallet had somehow fallen in there.

Bingo. There it was, half-hidden by something blue, maybe a scarf. She picked up the items to separate them and wished she hadn't.

The cloth wasn't a scarf. It was a blue turban with a dark hairpiece attached in the back. It had to be Kim's. Such a personal item, and he'd kept it. Alexis's eyes misted. He'd loved that woman with an enduring strength she could hardly imagine.

Intending to return it to the drawer, she began

to fold the turban neatly and heard a crackling sound. Inside the cap was a piece of paper, a small photograph. She stared at it for a long time, until she understood the image.

It was a picture of Kim and Dan together, both of them bald and smiling at the camera. He'd shaved his head to match hers. On the back was written, "I'm with you all the way." Dan's script.

Alexis had a lump in her throat, but she didn't understand why she grieved so deeply right then. Was it for the lovely couple—for the death of their innocent dreams? Or was it for the death of her own unreasonable, barely acknowledged ones? She studied the picture and saw true love. Dan and Kim Delito.

With shaky hands, she replaced the items in the drawer and put Dan's wallet on top of the coins in the ceramic dish. As she reentered the bedroom to retrieve her mobile from Dan's bed, she glanced at the wall in the reading alcove and lost her breath.

A large portrait—of her! Or what could have been her. Alexis sank onto the mattress, her heart pounding. No wonder everyone who knew Dan reacted strongly when they met her. No wonder the kids asked about "Auntie Kim's angel." At first glance, she and Dan's wife could have been sisters. She certainly looked more like Kim than Sherri.

At second glance, she saw the differences that Dan rattled off so easily. However, the resemblance left *her* rattled. Maybe the old saying about everyone having a double was true. She'd never thought about it before, never had reason to.

She slowly returned to her own bedroom, knowing she had to call Dan about his credit cards, and knowing she couldn't reveal a thing about her discovery or her state of mind. Dan had a game to play on Sunday. Besides, he already knew she and Kim resembled each other. It wouldn't shock him as it had her. She took a deep breath, hit the auto-dial and gave him the good news about the wallet.

"That's terrific, Ally. Thanks so much. You're a lifesaver."

"No problem."

"I'll see you late Sunday night. It's an early game."

"I'll be cheering."

They disconnected and she slumped against the headboard. After congratulating herself for pulling it off, she let the tears flow.

She'd always known, in her head, that Dan had loved Kim deeply. She'd known, too, about the resemblance between herself and Dan's late wife. But knowing something in your head and feeling it in your heart are two different things.

That was a lesson Alexis had learned the hard way when Sherri died. She'd seen it happen. She'd read the newspaper articles and the police reports. But it was only when she picked up the phone one day in mid-August to call her sister, and realized Sherri would never answer again, that she truly *understood*.

The emotions that washed over her now were as uncontrolled and strong as the feelings she hadn't been able to hold back on that summer afternoon. Alexis had always known, intellectually, that Dan was the wrong man for her. He still had an unknown relationship with the bottle. And he had an admitted habit of starting casual affairs with random women. She'd allowed herself to hope he'd kicked the booze and groupies. But even if he had, she now knew the one habit he'd never kick was Kim. And she also realized the only reason she herself had breached his defenses was that she reminded him of what he had lost.

She'd tried so hard to be rational, logical and sensible—all the qualities that had served her well in law school and the D.A.'s office. In fact, her rational mind had convinced her she could be just friends with Dan. That she didn't want anything more.

But if that were the case, admitting that no one would ever take Kim's place in his heart wouldn't hurt like a punch in the stomach. She wouldn't feel as though she had lost a vital battle she hadn't even conceded she was waging.

Her head dropped to her hands and she sobbed.

FEAR TRUMPED HER DISAPPOINTMENT when Dan was taken out of that Sunday's game at the beginning of the fourth quarter. This time, a brutal sacking left him on the ground, and Alexis held her breath when he didn't move for a long minute. Of course, he was surrounded by staff, who knelt next to him. While she watched, she saw him shake his head, then slowly manage to regain his feet. When the camera panned him, his grimace was clearly visible. The announcer said Delito had fallen directly on his right shoulder, his throwing arm, and was headed for some X-rays. The backup quarterback relieved him.

Silence descended on the game room as Dan's family watched along with her, watched their Danny-boy cradle his injured arm and walk slowly from the field accompanied by two staff members.

Anger and fear warred inside Alexis. "This is

the stupidest game ever invented, the dumbest way to earn a living. Why couldn't he have chosen a normal, safe job? He might get killed out there! And then where would Michelle be?"

"It could have been worse," said Rita, who didn't appear too happy, either. "It could have been a concussion."

"Look at the bright side," contributed Joe. "New England has a bye week coming up. No game next Sunday, so Dan'll have two weeks to recuperate."

"And that's supposed to make me happy?" snapped Alexis, jumping up from the sofa. "The same thing could happen again."

Joe shrugged, put up his hands. "Okay. You're right. I'm wrong. And stupid, too. Time for Joe to shut up."

She grabbed the remote and turned off the television. "I've seen enough."

"No, no, Ally. Put it back on. They'll give us updates on Dan's condition," said Rita.

She clicked the remote again to hear speculation about a shoulder separation.

"Don't expect him back tonight," said Nick. "They might treat him in New York."

"Just as well," grumbled Alexis. "Because when he walks through that door, I'm going to kill him myself."

But she didn't. Not when she heard his key jingle at midnight and ran downstairs. Not when he walked through the door with his arm in a sling, his tired eyes devouring her like a heat-seeking missile.

"Sorry to wake you, but I needed to be home. I needed to see you."

His words enveloped her with the warmth of a cozy blanket, and despite all her doubts, she quickly closed the distance between them. She stroked his cheek. "Welcome home, Danny-boy. But I think you should know that I hate football. I tried to like it, but I hate it. Just look at you. You're really hurt."

The corner of his mouth twitched as though he wanted to laugh—or kiss her. Resolutely, she stifled that thought.

"That's my spice girl. Never afraid to speak her mind. Don't be upset, Ally. I'll be just fine. I've got a lot of help."

He stepped to the side, and for the first time she saw he was not alone. "This is Bobby Siegel, a physical therapist with the team."

The guy was smaller than Dan, but still, that was no excuse to overlook someone. She hadn't noticed anybody but Dan in the entry hall. She shook the visitor's hand just as there was a soft rapping at the door.

"That's Louis," said Dan. "He'll take Bobby home after I'm iced down for the night. I didn't want to bother you to do it."

"And I'll be back early tomorrow," said the therapist, "to keep the ice going. The team doctor will be around to check Dan out again. And maybe Sean will show up, too."

"Or maybe not," said Dan. "He might be working hard with my backup."

As Alexis crossed the foyer to let Louis inside, she glanced from one man to the other, and the entire scene hit her as surreal. She'd gone down the rabbit hole and become part of a fantasy world peopled by folks who would never normally have crossed her path. A top-flight sports medicine team who knew their stuff. A talented professional coach who'd work with Dan step-by-step to get him back to full strength—so that he could return to the field and put himself in danger again.

"By the way," she said, leading the men into the kitchen, where the therapist loaded the freezer with a variety of ice packs, "who won the game? I never got to that part."

Identical grins spread across the faces of three grown men. "It was a good day," Dan said.

Welcome to the NFL.

It wasn't a happy thought.

CHAPTER TEN

THE BOSTON GLOBE—SPORTS
Monday, December 3
DELITO INJURED WITH SHOULDER
SEPARATION

With a season record to date of 13–1, New England's star QB is nursing a separated shoulder he received in yesterday's game against the Jets. A shoulder separation is usually a soft tissue or ligament injury to the junction between the collarbone and the shoulder.

"All appropriate treatments are being used to ensure a complete recovery," said Rick Thompson, head coach. "They include ice, immobilization and physical therapy, starting in a few days. The most important thing is to get Dan back to 100 percent. Luckily, he didn't fracture a bone."

When asked about Delito's chances of

playing in two weeks against the Titans, Thompson had no comment.

ALEXIS HAD PLENTY OF comments, especially after viewing the bruising of Dan's shoulder, but she kept all her opinions to herself. The game was Dan's business, after all, not hers. If he had tried to tell her how to prosecute a case, she would have told him where to get off. So she kept her mouth shut and tried to make sure he didn't reinjure himself accidentally, especially around Michelle, who got excited whenever she saw her daddy.

The ongoing activity in the house provided a distraction for her. With therapists, doctors and coaches in and out, with Maria preparing lunches and wanting her input, and with Michelle to care for, there was no opportunity to think about the Dan who lived in her heart, which was probably for the best.

"Are you going to your meeting tonight?" she asked on Wednesday afternoon when they were both in the game room with the baby. His arm was in a sling, he was downing anti-inflammatory medication, and she couldn't imagine him participating in anything with his customary get-up-and-go.

In his club chair, he shook his head. "I'm off

the hook. Wouldn't be able to concentrate much anyway."

"The pain's still bad, isn't it?" she asked.

Trying to shrug, he winced instead. "It's chronic. I'll be getting another cortisone shot tomorrow. That should ease it."

She bit her tongue to avoid talking about the chances of him playing on the sixteenth in Nashville. His fans were rooting for that to happen; he probably was, too. Not her. Enough was enough.

"I've missed you, Ally," he said quietly.

She understood the meaning behind his words but didn't want to follow up. "Missed me?" she protested. "I've been here 24/7 since you got home."

"And so have a million other people." He smiled. "One person seems like a million when all I've wanted is some time alone with you."

A corner of her heart tore, and she could have wept. Dan was simply confused. It was Kim he wanted. He'd shaved his head for her, had gotten drunk on their anniversary. Instead of crying, however, she averted her glance and said, "Dan—please don't go there. I'm a little off balance these days."

He studied her with his usual intensity. "What's going on? Oh, geez, Ally! It's football, isn't it? It's got you mixed up. Well, I won't be playing forever—I'm creeping up in years, and it's a young man's game."

"Creeping up?" She laughed in relief at his absurd conclusion. The man had more energy than anyone she'd ever met. "You're only thirty-one, so you're in for a long haul."

"Maybe, maybe not. But it's good to hear you laughing again. I love the sound." Suddenly, he yawned, and his eyes closed. "The chair is more comfortable than my bed."

"Then sleep here, if you can. I'll put Michelle down, too, and take a picture of you both. 'Father and Daughter—Naptime.'" She stood up and started toward the other side of the room, where Michelle was rolling around on her play mat.

"Very nice. But something's missing."

"What?"

"My good-night kiss."

Ally stopped short and almost stopped breathing. Had Dan decided he wanted to forego their agreement?

Memories of his kisses flooded her. The warmth of his skin. The electricity that had arced between them. It was so tempting to just give in. To say yes.

But if they were going to step past their self-imposed boundaries, they'd need to have a long, difficult talk first. About Kim. About the drinking. About the future. And Dan was in no condition for a serious talk that could distract him from his job.

"I'll have to owe you one," she said, retrieving the baby and taking her to the changing table. "Your daughter has priority."

"Only for now," he murmured.

Danny. Danny. Danny. Maybe he was genuinely trying to open himself up to a new life and a new love, but that new love couldn't be her. She ached for them both. They'd grown so close, laughing together, loving Michelle, but in the end, their relationship wouldn't work.

She wouldn't settle for second-best— which is exactly where she measured up against Kim Delito.

She wanted to be first. And that was a first. Never before in her adult life had she yearned to be so close to someone, so in sync, that they could laugh at the same jokes, share the same wonders and desire a life together.

Her old ways weren't working anymore, not with this man. And that was all the more reason to keep her distance.

DAN WISHED HE COULD be cloned. His career needed his full attention. He'd be flying to

Nashville with the team, not to play, but to provide support for his reserves. His backup would be the lead QB that weekend. Dan knew the player wanted to win for the team's sake, but more because he didn't want to let Dan down. The two weren't close friends, but Dan knew the younger man considered him a role model. It was hard to be someone's idol.

Ally also needed his full attention. She seemed to be walking on eggshells around him lately, always making general conversation, careful to avoid anything personal. He knew he was losing her. But why?

She was weirdly obsessed with keeping to their original agreement, a deal he'd half forgotten about until she reminded him of it the other day. He'd respect her wishes, of course, but he didn't know why she was insisting on sticking to a pact they'd made before they really knew each other. Before they'd kissed. Before they'd shared a home.

Was their life together really nothing more than business to her?

The idea gnawed at him like a persistent mosquito. He could swear she cared for him as more than her employer and Michelle's daddy. There were times he'd glimpsed the light of something more than friendship in her eyes.

But perhaps he was imagining it, because he wanted to see it so badly.

When she'd first appeared at his door, he'd assumed she was interested in him only for his money. In fact, he'd accused her of that very thing—and she'd looked a bit shamefaced, he had to admit.

Was he really nothing more than a checkbook to her? The idea appalled him, but he couldn't think of any other explanation for her coolness. He hadn't touched a drop of booze since the day they'd met. They'd rarely so much as raised their voices to each other.

But he knew Ally—at least, he thought he did—and he was convinced she wasn't as mercenary as he suspected. Whatever the reason for her detachment, it was making him miserable. He preferred the original Ally—the Ally who spoke her mind.

After he returned from Nashville, he'd instigate a conversation with Ally. He'd be able to continue his full-time recuperation at the stadium facilities, so the house would no longer be full of team staff. They'd be able to be themselves again.

On Friday, he hugged her at the door when Louis picked him up, and hope flowered when he felt her response and heard her parting words.

"No matter what happens in that game, Daniel, don't you dare—dare—dare put on a uniform." Stab, stab, stab. She still worried about him. A good sign.

"I'm on the disabled list, so I can't play. If we lose, we'd still lead the division anyway at 13–2. Of course, we'd need to win the final two games to have home field advantage for the play-offs. I'll be ready by then."

"Hmm…does this mean we're able to use the *S* word now?"

Her eyes twinkled, and she bit her lip trying to repress a smile, but the corners of her mouth lifted anyway.

"I suppose so," he replied, not hiding his grin at all. "But we'd still have to win the play-offs. I guess I can't fight it anymore. In the middle of December, the big game's on everyone's mind—that is, everyone who cares about this contest."

She made a disgruntled face and he hugged her again, kissed the baby and left the house without another word. Better to part on a happy note.

THEY LOST THE NASHVILLE game by one touch-down. On the plane, the medical staff and coaches worked out a dual therapy and practice schedule for Dan for the following week. In the car on the way home from the airport Sunday night, he fell asleep, and Louis had to wake him.

"You shoulda stayed home, Mr. Delito. Better off resting."

"You're probably right. Too bad the coach didn't ask your advice. Thanks for a smooth ride, Lou—not easy, with all the potholes. See you in the morning."

Dan walked to the front door, put his key in the lock and turned around. Louis was waiting for him to get inside, as though Dan were an invalid or a child. Or the starting quarterback for the New England Patriots. "I'm fine. Go home."

The other man waved and took off.

Dan stepped indoors and inhaled the lingering aroma of something baking, something sweet and delicious. He took another deep breath and tried to identify it. Chocolate-chip cookies? Alexis? That would be a sight. She'd never claimed to be a cook, and he'd never seen her elbow deep in meal prep in all the weeks she'd lived with him. Maybe Maria had come by earlier, or his mom.

Suddenly, his stomach growled, his fatigue lifted and he whistled his way down the hall. He'd soon sample whatever it was that smelled so good.

He stopped short in the kitchen doorway and stared at Christmas.

Garlands draped the walls and looped from the light fixtures. A tabletop tree sat on the counter, a bright Santa on the high chair's tray.

He hadn't bothered with the holiday in years. He stood frozen in place, sucker punched.

Ally was covered with flour. It was even in her hair, which was gathered at the back of her neck. An apron hadn't helped at all. She stood at the counter, humming as she checked the pages of an open book. Then she peeped into the oven.

"Potholders," he said, his voice gravelly. "Use potholders."

She whirled, hand on her heart. "Oh, my God, Danny. You scared me. I never heard a sound." Turning away, she grabbed the mitts, removed the cookie sheet and placed it on top of the stove.

He scanned the room again, trying to adjust to the upheaval. "What are you doing besides making a mess?"

Her forehead crinkled. "What does it look like? I'm getting us ready for Christmas. It's Michelle's first one."

"So what?" he asked. "She'll never remember it." He shrugged, glad to note the absence of pain in his shoulder. But his heart twisted when he saw the hurt on her face. She pressed her lips together, came closer and clasped his arms. Then she looked straight up at him. Gazing into those soft green eyes, he felt himself begin to drown.

"I know Michelle won't remember," she whispered, "but the point is that you'll remember. I'll remember, too. You'll take pictures and share them with her later on. You'll build memories. Create photo albums. Like in a real family." She waved toward the fridge. "See, you've already got pictures of her here and all over the house, like…like a real family is supposed to have of their children."

She averted her gaze. A suspicion began to grow in Dan's mind.

"Would this happen to be your first Christmas celebration, too?" he whispered.

A rosy blush blossomed from her neck to her face. "Let's just say it will be my happiest one."

Placing his finger under her chin, he said, "Look at me again."

She slowly raised her eyes, and he was stunned at her shyness. So unusual for Alexis Brown.

"Then we'll do it. We'll have the biggest, merriest Christmas right here." Not for the baby's sake, but for Ally's.

Ally, the woman he loved. Even if she didn't love him—yet.

The warmth of her smile made his blood

sizzle. Jumping her bones seemed like a great idea, but it wasn't going to happen. Not at the moment, anyway. Instead, he tried to keep the conversational ball rolling.

"Fair warning, Ally. I'm way out of practice with all this stuff." He gestured at the decorations.

Her bright expression turned to one of concern, and she patted his arm. "I think I understand. For a man who doesn't have a picture of his wife on display anywhere except in his own bedroom, I can imagine you certainly didn't have the heart for Christmas in recent years."

He paused, confused. Where was she going with this? "What brought that up?"

"I wasn't prying, Dan. I saw the portrait when I searched for your wallet," Ally said.

Was the discovery of that picture related to Ally's coolness last week? If so, how?

"When I saw it," Ally continued, "I nearly passed out, and I certainly understood your family's reaction to meeting me. Then I wondered why I hadn't seen any shots of her before. I wondered if I'd been unconsciously oblivious, so I searched the other rooms and…"

"And you found none because there aren't any on display." He pulled out a chair for Ally and sat down facing her. He took her hand. "Hiding family pictures wasn't my call. It was Kim's. As the cancer ripped through her, she couldn't bear seeing herself from the good days, so—"

"So you put them all away."

"Yeah, I did."

She squeezed his hand.

"You were a wonderful husband," she said.

"Not as wonderful as you are for putting up with everything." He came with a lot of baggage that was still weighing him down. Right now, for example, with their talk about Kim's illness, Ally had unknowingly ignited his trigger. He felt the urge, the beads of sweat beginning to break out on his skin.

He wanted a drink.

SHE WATCHED HIM SNATCH two chocolate-chip cookies from the tray, pour himself a tall glass of milk and down it without pause while standing at the refrigerator. Then, he bit into a cookie, the result of her very first attempt at baking. Stunned that he'd consider such frivolous carbs, she watched him chew, pause, then close his eyes—tasting and measuring—hopefully, savoring the flavor. When he finally swallowed and sighed with pleasure, a glow of satisfaction warmed her. Another first for her. She rarely cooked for others, but Dan's appreciation made her think of trying other cookie recipes she'd found.

"Delicious," he said, biting into the second one. "I've heard chocolate is a heavenly flavor, and I totally agree."

"You probably haven't had any in ten years," Alexis said, "so you're in love with it now. But thanks for the compliment. It means a lot to me."

He beckoned with his finger. "Come here a minute."

Curious, she went.

"See that?" he asked, pointing overhead. "Glad you remembered the mistletoe."

She hadn't noticed any mistletoe among the greenery but didn't argue. Didn't want to argue. She was tired of being cautious and responsible. Dan had demons, and one day she might well have to confront them. But it was Christmas, and she deserved a reward after this harrowing year. One kiss couldn't hurt. Could it?

As soon as his lips touched hers, she knew she'd been fooling herself. One kiss would never be enough. Kissing Dan was everything she remembered from the last time and more. When he held her in his arms, it was the only place she wanted to be.

"You are much better than any wine," he

murmured, deepening the kiss to an intimacy she'd never known. An intimacy laced with hunger, yearning and need. His need, her need. She met him with a joy she'd never experienced before. A revelation about giving and receiving love.

In a quicksilver moment, however, a hint of loss pierced her delight. But still, she pressed against him to receive a dozen kisses on her neck, her cheek, behind her ear. Kisses that made her shiver and ignore the future.

"I want to make love with you," he whispered, "real love. You're in my blood, you're in my mind all day long. Every night, I think about coming home to you—and I can't wait."

He was lonely, she thought. He was a good man, a wonderful man, a man who'd turned his world upside down for the sake of his daughter. A man she now believed had given up the bottle for good. A man who was lonely for his wife. And she loved him.

"But I won't break my promise to you," he continued. "You're safe in this house. No strings."

Her response was instinctive, as natural to her as breathing. "I absolve you of your promise."

The warmth in his eyes turned to heat mixed with equal amounts of anticipation and wonder. His hand trembled when he reached for hers. Weaving her fingers through his, she followed him.

Not to his bedroom where Kim's picture hung.

Not to her bedroom across from the baby.

But up, up to the top floor, to the guest suite with the balcony overlooking the beautiful city.

"Just for us," he said quietly, turning on a lamp.

Relief flowed through her. The suite was virgin territory for both of them in this house. No shadows here.

When he faced her again, his eyes caressed her, hot and lethal, but he seemed afraid to move. "Ally?"

She took a single step toward him, his arms opened, and she was there. A shower of kisses rained down on her, and her pulse roared in her ears. There was something about this man that turned her to mush, and she wanted more.

He eased her onto the bed, and slowly, as if drawing out both the pleasure and pain of waiting, one garment at a time landed on the floor. Hers. His. She was Eve to his Adam, exploring and discovering, as no two people had ever done before them, enjoying everything that made them human. With Dan, she traveled a new road in an exotic world, so much different than the one she'd visited during her failed college love affair.

"It's been a l-long time—" What was he doing?

Her breasts swelled and her nipples hardened as his tongue circled each one and glided across the peaks. Her breath caught in jagged gasps, and her legs became restless. He covered them with his own.

"It's more fun this way," he said.

Fun? She was dying of pleasure. Especially when he leaned over and breathed his warmth onto the moist folds between her thighs. Tension mounted and coiled inside her. She wanted to burst as he fondled her. "Oh, my… Dan, Dan…"

"Go for it, sweetheart, go for it."

A wonderful idea. She closed her eyes, blocking all distractions. His teasing strokes made her tighter, every gentle breath brought her closer, another brushstroke…and one more…. She was so close… Oh, yes! She erupted. Hit the edge and vaulted over. Tremors racked her body, lifting her from the bed.

"That's it, love, that's it."

She heard the joy in his voice, the joy he took in giving her pleasure, and she reached blindly for him, her legs parting. Receiving wasn't enough. She wanted to give. Give to him what he'd given to her.

"Come to me, Danny-boy."

"I'll be all yours, in one second."

She heard a ripping sound, saw the condom. And then he was all hers, as he'd promised.

He entered her with care, waited for her signal, for her hips to lift before he thrust a little harder, and a little harder still.

"Oh, yes." She wrapped her arms around him. "Don't pull back…"

So he thrust faster, and she met him full on.

Beneath her fingers, the muscles on Dan's back remained rigid. Tension grew inside her again like a tightly wound spring.

They exploded together.

"Touchdown," he whispered. "With a point-after thrown in."

"If this is what a touchdown feels like, I'll love the game forever."

Keep it light, she thought, because forever wasn't for them. She was a realist. Their relationship would end at some point. It had to. Despite the love for him that grew daily, despite the heat that raced through her with every thought of him, and despite the warmth and affection she received from him, it wasn't enough.

She would not become a second Mrs. de Winter, never quite able to replace the first. She wanted no ghostly Rebecca haunting her.

But she would enjoy the moment, enjoy the

attention and care of a man who tried hard to do the right thing for the people in his life, especially for his daughter. Living in the moment was worth the price she'd pay later.

"I HEAR ALEXIS HATES the game," said Sean Callan.

Dan had just gotten out of the shower in the locker room at the stadium and was partly dressed in street clothes when he heard his coach's voice.

"Yeah? Who says?"

"A little birdie."

That could describe any of the half-dozen people who had been in and out of Dan's house since the injury. Dan reached for his pants, pulled them on, straightened his shirt. The source didn't really matter. Putting out fires did.

"Sure, Ally got upset about the shoulder, but she doesn't hate the game." At least, he didn't think so. "In fact, she has a new respect for it." He smiled as he remembered their conversation about touchdowns.

Ally couldn't hate the game. Not really. Not when he loved it so much. Football had gotten him through some of the worst times of his life, and he'd enjoyed some of the best times playing the game, as well. Simply staring at a one-hundred-yard field of grass got him excited. Nah, don't borrow trouble. Ally was overreacting.

"I hope you know what you're talking about, Dan. Your recovery has been great, and today's practice with the line was all we could hope for. We want everything to keep running smoothly. And that includes the thoughts in your head." The coach stared at him hard. "Know what I mean?"

Dan knew exactly what he meant. The game was as much mental as it was physical. Only the tough survived. Well, he'd survived so far, even with a couple of bad detours a few years ago.

"My head's in a good place," said Dan. "She put up a Christmas tree. It was nice."

Callan's eyes bulged. "Nice? Sounds damned serious to me. But if you've got any big plans, now's not the time. We're looking at some critical football coming up."

Dan nodded. He had big plans, all right, and Ally was their name. Their lovemaking had settled his few remaining doubts. Ally was one-in-a-million. Beneath her assertive, firecracker exterior was a heart full of love—for him. And, of course, Michelle. Christmas Day would be a perfect time for a proposal.

Whistling cheerfully, he headed out for his regular Wednesday evening appointment.

ALEXIS COULDN'T BEAR TO watch the offensive plays against the Steelers that Sunday during game sixteen. Dan was back at work, involved in every action. Which meant that each time he received the ball from his center, Pittsburgh's defensive line made his life miserable. They went after him like predators. Sure, it was their job to take him out, to exploit his possible weakness after an injury. She understood that intellectually, but hid her eyes just the same.

In the family suite at the stadium, she wouldn't allow the baby to watch, either. It made no sense—Michelle, at five months old, understood nothing—but Alexis didn't care. Nick, Joe and Larry shook their heads; Rita smiled with understanding and closed her eyes a few times, too, and the younger women just seemed delighted. Alexis knew they were reading a special meaning into her actions. To them, she was the key to Dan's happier life. She couldn't help knowing they were rooting for her and Dan as a couple.

There was no point in disillusioning them before it was necessary. With more football games yet to be played and the holiday festivities demanding attention, everyone was busy enough.

New England was in the lead at halftime. Dan's bullet arm was back. His quick ball release to his receivers sailed true, anticipating where they'd be, but Alexis's nerves were shot. Her clothes were actually damp with perspiration.

"Hey, Ally. Our boy's in great shape, so you can relax. Besides, it's only a game."

Since when? Dan's brother could barely refrain from doing a happy dance, he was so elated with the team's performance. But she supposed Joe had offered all the comfort he was capable of giving.

"Relaxing is not that easy," she said.

"What if he was a cop? Or a firefighter?" asked Theresa. "You'd have a breakdown every morning."

"True." But she knew a little something about law enforcement. "Do you know which profession has one of the highest, if not *the* highest, divorce rate?"

No one replied.

"Police officer. The regular police force. I rest my case. This is crazy."

Dan's family looked so comically forlorn on hearing this new information that she had to bite her lip to keep from laughing. She decided to give them a break.

"The good part is," she continued with all eyes on her, "that Dan absolutely loves what he does. I know that. It's just..." She sighed without finishing the sentence. She'd never get used to Dan's chosen profession. To all the risk.

"Don't be scared," said Mary Ann. "Get mad instead. It's much healthier."

Get mad? At whom? At people who were doing their jobs? Doing what they were paid to do? It didn't make much sense. It would be like getting angry at teachers for teaching or bartenders who served alcohol. It was their job.

And that's what she continued to tell herself throughout the third quarter, each of the three times Dan was sacked and her heart almost stopped.

At the beginning of the fourth quarter, when New England was up by fourteen, Nick took the seat next to Alexis, stretched his legs and leaned back as though he'd sit for a spell. An unusual sight. Dan's father spent almost the entire game on his feet cheering, yelling, giving directions, enjoying every minute. Undoubtedly, he had a reason for this personal visit, and Alexis waited.

"I've been thinking," he began, "that you don't know much about football—about the game itself or what it takes to get to the professional level. Am I right?"

She almost laughed. As if she'd had time for football when she was younger. She'd been hell-bent on making the honor roll, looking out for Sherri, outmaneuvering Cal and controlling her anger at Peggy for staying with him.

Football and other extracurricular activities had been for regular kids, kids with good families, kids who had time for play. They weren't for kids like her, the ones with chronic stomachaches. None of this was Nick's business, however, so she kept her response light.

"You could be right, Nick. I don't have a brother, so maybe my knowledge of football is superficial." She bestowed a quick smile on him, and bounced Michelle on her lap. "Why do I have the feeling you're about to correct that?"

"Because I am. But we can't do it all today." No more lounging for Nick. He sat up straight and looked at her head-on with dark brown eyes so reminiscent of Dan's. "For today, I just want you to understand one thing, Ally. And it's the real deal. It's important."

The older man fidgeted and his voice was tight. Whatever he had to say was as serious as the Super Bowl to him. She paid attention.

"You can teach a quarterback many things, such as making good decisions or dealing with pressure," said Nick, "but you can't teach him how to throw the ball just exactly right—it's an unnatural movement. You can't teach that quick release that separates a good quarterback from a great one. A man either has the innate talent or he doesn't."

He looked toward the field and pointed at the players. "The great ones are born, Ally. They're not made." He paused for a moment, then asked, "Understand what I'm saying about my son?"

He wasn't bragging. He was giving her facts. Enough information to lift the mist. Her aha moment had arrived. "I think I do," she whispered. "You're saying Dan is one of the special ones?"

"And that's not a father speaking," Nick said, confirming her thoughts. "Read about him. About his work, not the gossip." He reached for his granddaughter and went to watch the game with Rita.

Ally's mind raced. Dan's career was as much a calling to him as music was to Elton John or art had been to Jackson Pollock. It defined who he was. Dan and football were synonymous.

But why hadn't she understood that earlier? He'd been with New England for some years now. She was living with the man, for crying out loud. She'd seen how strict he was with himself. Football was his career, and he loved it. Period. It was a fact. She always dealt in facts. What was different in this case?

Her gaze traveled through the suite and landed

on Michelle. Had Alexis hoped he'd give up the dangerous game because he had a precious child now? Yeah, maybe. Maybe she'd hoped against hope that this would be his last season.

That wasn't going to happen. So, if she was to remain a friend of this family after she left Dan's house, she needed an attitude adjustment.

She rose from her seat and joined the rest of the clan. The team was twenty yards from goal. Dan caught the snap, dropped back, tried to pass the ball and was tackled by five Steelers.

She clenched her fists. "Get your friggin' hands off him," she yelled, ready to pound the glass wall. "You overweight sacks of squalid slop!" Man, that felt good.

"Whoo-hoo," cried Mary Ann. "Listen to the classy lady. Didn't I tell you that mad was better than scared?"

"And you were damn right."

CHAPTER ELEVEN

THE BOSTON GLOBE—SPORTS
Monday, December 24
DAN'S THE MAN
SEASON STANDS AT 14–2
SUPER BOWL FEVER BUILDS
A flawless performance by Dan Delito yesterday puts the Pats one game away from the AFC's Eastern Division title. Despite his recent injury, Delito handled an aggressive defense by the Steelers, passing for 259 yards with no interceptions. He ruled the game….

DAN FINISHED THE ARTICLE, folded the paper and put it on the kitchen counter for Ally, who'd warned him last night not to throw it out as he usually did or she'd order a duplicate subscription. Her threat made an impression. Ally didn't waste money. She clipped coupons for Maria; she explained her own purchases for the baby to Dan as though she was apologizing. So, two newspaper subscriptions? Very un-Ally-like.

The story about the game, in fact, was good for his ego and would have gone to his head if it weren't for his aches and pains. Last night's had been a tough contest. No doubt about it. Afterward, he'd ridden home with Ally and Michelle and soaked in his own hot tub until he could almost move without groaning.

He'd been about to get out of the water when Ally showed up in his basement training area and removed her robe.

Long shapely legs topped with dark silky panties. Above that, a matching silk bra. He sank back onto the hot tub's bench, perfectly happy to remain where he was.

"The baby's down for the night, and I thought maybe you'd like some company," she said, stepping into the tub.

"Maybe?" His voice cracked. "There's no question about it, sweetheart, if the company is you."

He watched her blush as she lowered herself slowly into the hot water. "A beautiful mermaid," he whispered.

"A funny mermaid," she said, dimpling up at him, "who doesn't know how to swim."

"Then I'll teach you. After the season, we

can take a vacation. Maybe Florida or the Bahamas."

"Well, that would be nice, except for one tiny inconvenience. With some luck, I'll be working. As in fully employed elsewhere and off your payroll."

Not if life followed the path he hoped for. But he didn't want to argue with her then. Instead, they soaked for a while, holding hands, stroking, touching. Then they showered off the chlorine and explored each other with healing massages. And made love in ways that didn't require a condom.

But afterward, she wouldn't sleep with him in his bed.

"You have to be comfortable, Dan. You need a purely restful night."

What she said was true, but he couldn't help feeling she was holding back. The intimacy they'd shared should have continued through the night, with legs intertwined now and then, a hand reaching out from time to time. The way loving couples slept. The real reason for separate bedrooms was something she wouldn't share.

He thought about the sparkling ring he'd brought home last Wednesday night, after his appointment. A perfect diamond to be sure, but not glitzy or huge enough to make Ally uncomfortable. He thought she'd like a traditional round setting, but he'd change it in a heartbeat if she said the word. Maybe when she found it under the tree tomorrow, and he proposed to her, any remaining doubts she had would fade away.

He was prepared to handle the biggest argument she could present: Michelle. Ally might think his marriage proposal was because of the baby. Their arrangement was so convenient; they lived like a little family already. Ironically, however, his daughter had nothing to do with his feelings for Alexis.

He imagined a kaleidoscope of Ally's everyday life—feeding the baby, greeting him at the door, talking on the phone, baking cookies with flour in her hair. Full of energy. A woman who loved hard, with courage, and whose personal sweetness always triumphed over her defenses. A woman who had tried to do the right thing from the time she was a child herself, regardless of the pain or expense she might incur. Was it any wonder he'd fallen in love with Ally?

Please, God, let her say yes.

THE SEVEN-FOOT-HIGH FIR tree dominated the game room. Early on Christmas morning, Ally stood in the doorway, as she'd done every day during the last week, and felt a thrill just looking at the majestic tree and all the colorful decorations. Dan had helped in his spare time, tossing tinsel in what he called his "free-form" style, while she savored the symmetry of the ornaments she'd hung. Never before had she trimmed such a beauty, and never before had she looked forward to sharing the spirit of the day with people she loved as much as Michelle and Dan.

Except for Sherri. She should be here, too, celebrating and loving Michelle. *Your daughter is happy, darling. I promise.*

Alexis tried to regain control. It wasn't easy. Finally she focused on the gifts and saw a few additions to yesterday's pile. Dan must have been busy at the last minute. Not her. Although most people complained about it, shopping had proven as much fun as decorating the tree. In the last two weeks, she'd wrapped all her presents with delight. She was anticipating a lovely day, and was especially eager to see Dan's reaction to the gifts she'd created for him.

"Can't wait, can you? Just like a kid."

The man in her thoughts appeared behind her wearing jeans and a T-shirt, and holding Michelle, who wriggled against her daddy like a tiny, battery-operated baby doll.

"I can't wait to watch Michelle play with—

or eat, or smack, or destroy—her presents," she replied. "But it will have to wait for later, when she's not fussing. Come to the kitchen. She's hungry."

Alexis started for the stairs. "Oh, did you change her?"

"Of course! That's the first thing we did. Right, petunia?" He kissed his daughter on her belly. "Can't have you a soggy mess and getting a rash, can we?"

Michelle gurgled and vocalized as though having a real conversation with her daddy. Alexis's heart warmed at their continually growing relationship.

"I'm so proud of you, Dan. You're not a rookie anymore. You're handling Michelle like a pro, as if you've done it with a dozen other children."

"Aw, shucks, ma'am," he said with a wink. "She's just like a little ol' football—that can't be thrown or dropped."

Her compliment had gotten to him. His ruddy face, his attempt at humor. He was embarrassed. She patted his arm. "You'll be fine when you're on your own. I know she's in good hands now."

His complexion paled, and she said quickly, "But I'm ten minutes away if you need me. Anytime at all."

He nodded in silence. After they entered the kitchen, Dan continued to hold the baby while Ally prepared the rice cereal.

"Bib's on her high chair. Do you want to feed her since you're available today, or shall I?" she asked.

"I love making a mess," he said. "Let me at it."

Such everyday conversation, she thought. So lovely, so intimate.

He propped Michelle in her chair, and a moment later, Ally gave him the cereal but placed the bottle out of the baby's sight. "Don't let her see it until she eats a few spoonfuls."

"Gotcha."

Ally had just crossed the kitchen to start the daily pot of coffee when she heard Dan say, "Hang on a sec, Ally. Come here and look at this."

She raced back to them.

"Look and listen," Dan said. He put a bit of cereal on Michelle's spoon, fed it to her and then tapped her bottom gum. Click, click, click. "She's got a tooth!"

A huge grin split his face. His eyes gleamed. His whole being exuded joy. The man looked as though no other baby in the entire world had ever gotten a first tooth.

Her heart melted yet again, drop by drop, as

Dan revealed once more the essence of who he was—a devoted dad to a child he'd known for less than three months.

Ally would never love another man the way she loved Dan Delito.

"FORGET ABOUT ALL THE PRICEY stuff," Dan said to Ally an hour later in the game room, "just give her lots of tissue paper."

Michelle was having a ball exploring colorful ribbons and bows, slapping at paper and ignoring all the gifts inside the boxes. The picture she made was totally adorable and cameraworthy. Ally took one shot after another.

"I hope some of them are even half as fabulous as the subject matter," she said.

Dan lay flat on the floor now, faceup, the baby prone on his stomach. Drool landed on his shirt, one little hand slapped his chest, and then Michelle's bottom rose as she used her toes to push herself forward toward his chin.

"Go, baby, go," Ally encouraged, snapping away. "She'll be crawling soon. I'm going to babyproof this house before I leave. Outlets, stairs, fireplaces—goodness, there's a lot of potential hot spots for a baby."

"But not today," said Dan, sitting up. "Today is for celebrating—and I see some more presents waiting to be opened before we head out to my folks'."

That was the plan. A private morning and a family afternoon. He watched Ally scurry to the base of the tree. "I've got something for you, Dan. I hope you like it."

She sounded nervous about it. Silly woman. "Of course I'm going to like it," he said as he walked toward her, holding the baby, and then sat down on the floor. "I'm going to love it no matter what it is, so relax."

"Actually, it's from Michelle and me." She gave him the gaily wrapped square package, then gripped her hands together while he began to tear the paper away with Michelle's help.

"Then I'm going to doubly like it," he said, his curiosity rising as more of the present was exposed.

Awesome. He wouldn't have to fake a reaction at all, but for some reason, his voice wouldn't work. In his hands was a colorful homemade scrapbook with the title: Michelle's Playbook for Daddy. It was a work of art and creativity.

He slowly turned the pages, trying to take it all in. Ally had used a potpourri of color, design and materials, and best of all, she'd interspersed photos of the baby with the text. Each topic started a new page and was presented as though it were written by Michelle.

He gazed at the woman who'd created this special gift for him, this labor of love. "I'm speechless. I can't even imagine how many hours must have gone into this. It's beautiful, Ally, and something I'll keep forever."

Her cheeks were on fire. "I guess Michelle had a lot to say."

He opened to the first page, which was entitled: Waking Up. He read:

Hi Daddy!
When I wake up in the morning, I need lots of kisses and raspberries and giggles. We need to start the day happy. After you kiss me all over, you can change my soggy dia-per. Don't forget to use the wipes and salve for my bottom. And throw the diaper in the special pail. I don't want a stinky room!
Love and XXXX,
Michelle
P.S. Any questions? Call Auntie Ally.

"This is fantastic," he said. "You've even listed the baby products on the bottom of the page."

Her eyes shone like green marble, her smile wide. "I'm so glad you like it. After all, I want to be sure you know what you're doing with my niece!"

After I leave.

He understood all too well the words she didn't say, and his mouth became dry. His time had come. She had no idea that, however nervous she had been about giving her gift to him, he was ten times more anxious about what he was going to do next. But he tried to act cool.

"Ally? See that box with the big red bow?"

She nodded.

"For you. From me."

While she retrieved it, he put Michelle into her swing and set it in motion before sitting down again. He patted the floor next to him when Ally returned.

She sat down and began unwrapping. A smaller second box was inside the first. Then a third was inside the second, each one wrapped and tied.

"Oh, Dan. You're making me work for my gift. It's like those Russian nesting dolls."

"Sure." As if he knew what those were.

She was really into it, having fun like a kid. This Christmas was surely the best holiday she'd ever had. So maybe he'd made a mistake with the ring. Maybe he should have waited and given her lots of regular presents to open instead of muddying the waters.

Too late now. She'd reached the smallest package and was eagerly untying the petite bow. She ripped the wrapping paper and stared at the blue velvet box for a moment, then glanced toward him, a crease growing across her forehead. In the pit of his stomach, he knew he'd blown it.

"Dan?" she whispered.

He covered her hands with his own. "I love you, Ally. It's as simple as that. I think about you all the time, daytime, nighttime, at home, at a game, you're always with me. And—and I was hoping we—we could make a life together. Because, I just love you. And if my hands are sweating, I'm sorry."

"Oh, Dan."

Horrified at the tears that rolled down her cheeks—not tears of joy, he was pretty sure— he scooped her onto his lap.

"Don't cry, please don't cry."

She'd buried her head against his shoulder, her weight against him, arms around him. Full of trust. Love. He thought he understood that much, but was otherwise confused as hell. He'd figure it out later. Now, he held her, cuddled her. Kissed her. The next move, however, had to be Ally's.

She handed him the unopened box. "I can't accept this, Danny, no matter how much I'm tempted."

That sounded promising, but there was no script in his playbook for this. He'd have to punt.

"Do you love me, Ally?"

"I—I do," she whispered. "Of course I do."

His heart soared. Confidence returned. He could do this—he was good at improvising. As long as she loved him, anything was possible.

"Talk to me, Ally," he said softly while brushing kisses on her temple.

He saw her chest heave, heard her huge sigh. "Remember the weekend you were away, and I saw Kim's picture in your bedroom?"

"Uh-huh."

"Well, I also saw another picture, a small one of you and her together, when she was very sick. You had shaved your head."

His lids snapped shut. He remembered when that photo was taken—during the worst of times. "And?" he pursued.

"I could see how much you loved her. I knew it the first time I met you, when you were stinking drunk. You and Kim were so tight—a once-in-a-lifetime kind of love."

Oh, God. He knew where she was going with this now, but he didn't stop her. He wanted to know everything on her mind. She turned her head, and he saw the tears.

"I cried for you the night I found that picture. I cried for her, too. And then I cried for me."

"No, Ally, no. There's no need to cry. I love you."

"I believe you care. That you have true…affection. So let's just continue as we are. What do they call it nowadays? Friends with benefits?"

"What?" he cried, not believing his ears. "That's not good enough! It's an insult to us both. I want more than that." He caught his breath, spoke softer. "Ally, sweetheart, I want to come home to you every night and hold you in my arms, I want to share laughs, go on long walks—everything that's part of an honest, full-time marriage."

But she was shaking her head before he'd finished speaking. "I'm sorry, Dan. Truly sorry. But I won't be—I *cannot* be—second-best, and that's what a marriage to you would be like. Kim would be in the house with us."

"Then we'll get another house."

"She'd be there, too. She was your true love. Not I."

Silence reverberated in the room, while he wrapped his mind around all her assumptions. Did a joyful life have to end with Kim? In a long-ago time, he'd thought it did, but not anymore. How could he make Ally understand?

"No one, Ally, should settle for being second-best. Not you, and not me. You're right about Kim and me having a great marriage, a wonderful relationship. It's exactly because of that marriage that I know what I'm missing—and I want it again!

"I want to live again. I want to love again. And with you, my wonderful, sweet tigress, I would not be settling for second-best. My heart pumps love, sweetheart. Lots and lots of love."

She twisted around in his lap, looked at him with tears still running down her beautiful face. "Every woman in love wants to be first."

"Deserves to be first," he added, "and you are first simply by being uniquely you."

She settled back against his chest, which was still so constricted it hurt to breathe. "You're killing me here, Ally."

"Oh, sorry. I'll move."

If he didn't laugh, he'd cry. "Stay where you are, woman, and just answer my question."

"And what would that be?" But now, a tiny twinkle shone in her eyes, and he brought her close and kissed her once, twice, then again and again. She didn't object.

"Will—you—marry—me?" The words between kisses were the best he could do.

"Yes—I—will." Seemed Ally couldn't do any better than he.

They laughed together. "I'm a happy man today. Thank you, Ally."

Her tears threatened again. She wasn't a barracuda at all. Just a sweet family goldfish.

His future looked bright, blessed with all the joy and noise of family, including a woman he loved with his whole heart. He placed the ring on her finger. A perfect fit.

Dear God, please let it last this time. Let the beautiful promise be fulfilled. Amen.

TRAVELING WITH MICHELLE WAS both an art and a science, and they were only going to Dan's parents' place. Ally hoisted the stuffed diaper bag from the floor of the baby's room and slipped the strap over her shoulder. Amazing how one little baby required so much stuff.

She started down the flight of stairs, stealing glances at the ring on her finger. Dan had understood her hesitation. He hadn't dismissed her fears with trite explanations. Later, he'd encouraged her to resume her career whenever the time was right—for her. He was tender, warm and sweet, a man who knew how to love. And she loved him back, one hundred percent. She had no doubts at all. He was no Calvin Brown.

Dan and Michelle were bundled up for winter and waiting for her at the front door with shopping bags full of gifts to bring with them. As she descended the last flight, she heard, "What is taking your mommy so long?"

The *M* word. So beautiful. "I'll have to adopt her."

Dan cricked his neck back. "So file the papers, and do it faster than you pack a bag. We're sweating in these clothes."

But his grin belied his complaint, and as soon as she came abreast of them, he said, "You are gorgeous." And he kissed her.

"Ready for the hordes?" he asked, opening the door.

"I wish you'd warned them, you know, about us." Not for their sakes, but for hers. She liked his family but still wasn't used to crowds or to a fuss being made. Wasn't used to twelve people talking at once. And what if they weren't happy about the engagement? How would that affect Dan?

She stepped outside to threatening skies. "Looks like snow coming."

"Then let's get started."

Ten minutes later they were finally packed into the big car, with Dan behind the wheel, and on their way to Rita and Nick's.

"It's not too late," said Dan as they entered the highway.

"Too late for what?"

He spoke his mom's name aloud for his hands-free car phone, and a moment later Rita's voice came through the system.

"Hi, Mom. It's Dan. We're on our way. Need anything last minute?"

When he glanced at Ally in question, she whispered, "Give her a heads-up."

"Ah, one more thing, Mom. Yeah. Ally and I have something to tell everyone. Something good. So crack open a bottle of ginger ale."

That's all it took for Rita to start screaming for Nick, and Dan disconnected. "Feel better now?"

"Yes." But the dancing butterflies were having a ball in her stomach.

"Anything else on your mind?" he asked.

"Like a million things."

"Such as?"

"The tabloids will have a field day smashing your reputation again. Maybe mine, too." She sighed and bit her thumbnail. "I don't like that."

"Who cares? The legit papers will get it right. What else?"

She thought about it. A different house? A new job? Life during the off-season? It was too much to think about at once.

"We'll figure it out as we go along," she said. "It's the only way to handle it all."

"That's my girl, going with the flow."

She was his girl for the entire visit. He was either at her side, or searching for her, or meeting her gaze across a crowded room. Her gaze and her smile.

"You've been smiling all day," Dan said, sliding up beside her after dinner.

"Well, life is good. Your family's been great."

Until Rita asked about the wedding as they cleaned up the kitchen.

"We haven't gotten that far yet," said Ally. "But certainly after the season's over. Way over."

Rita nodded. "We know your sister's gone, honey, but we'd love to meet the rest of your family. I can invite them to dinner."

Ally shook her head. "Not in a million years. Cal and Peggy are so *not* in my life, it's better you think of me as an orphan."

Rita frowned. "I don't understand. Won't they want to come to the wedding?"

"Drop it, Mom. She won't invite them. Heck, I won't invite them," said Dan, as he brought in more dirty dishes from the dining room. "Her father's a lifelong alcoholic. Her mother does what he says. Both are totally irresponsible. In fact, Ally wound up paying for all of Sherri's burial expenses."

"The subject's now dropped," said Rita,

standing up and hugging Ally. "No more talk about your family. It's you who are special. You're a wonderful woman, a strong woman, and we count our blessings that you knocked on Dan's door. Welcome to our family, Alexis."

Tears threatened to spill onto Ally's cheeks. Rita's lovely words of praise and approval had surprised her. She'd waited thirty-one years to be warmed by such support from a special woman. From a mother. If it couldn't be her own, Dan's mom would do.

Just as Ally would do for Michelle.

CHAPTER TWELVE

"WAIT INSIDE WHILE I clean off the car."

Dan left Ally in the doorway of his parents' house and jogged to the curb with the baby's travel bag, which he threw into the SUV. He and his brother had shoveled the front path and sidewalk a few minutes ago. Now, he heard the sound of snowplows in the near distance clearing the roads.

A white Christmas, all right. Snow had continued to fall quietly all day, resulting in a five-inch accumulation so far. His nephews and nieces had piled into the back-yard after dinner, first building a snowman, then pelting each other with snowballs. That's when the adults joined in, taking the fun to a new level, causing shrieks from the kids to echo in the air.

He'd had a lot of fun just playing with the family, but more important, Ally had had a great day. His family had welcomed her, Mary Ann and Theresa were generous with their hugs. Ally would have some more new friends in addition to Roz.

Sprinkled with snow, he returned to his "women."

"Ready to go?"

"Definitely. This baby is so off schedule."

He kissed her and tried not to laugh. She was very Ally with her schedules. "I'll take Michelle, and you can hold on to my jacket."

"Hon-ey," she said, drawing the word out. "Look, I'm wearing boots. I can walk on my own."

"But you're spoiling all my fun," he complained. "I'm the big he-man, remember?"

"Ah. Little woman. Big man." She pointed to herself and to him. "Almost forgot."

He enjoyed their bantering until they were strapped into the car and on the street, watching the snow hit the windshield. Ally became quiet, tacitly acknowledging his need to concentrate on the road.

"It's not too bad," Dan said, after driving several blocks toward the highway. "Unless there's black ice on the ground already, which I doubt, we'll be fine."

"These side roads haven't been plowed yet, so either you're a great driver or this is a safe car."

Her words sounded confident, but her hands gripped each other, turning her fingers white. He would have rolled his eyes if he'd dared. Ally knew nothing about automobiles, wouldn't know a "safe" car from a lousy one, didn't even have a driver's license. As she'd explained to him several times, a city-dwelling pedestrian with access to great public transportation doesn't need a car. Investing in her condo made much more sense. He wouldn't argue that.

"This car," she said now, looking around the spacious interior and cooing at Michelle in the backseat, "is like having a little tank around us."

"You're in a Lexus four-wheel drive SUV, sweetheart. My winter vehicle."

"Winter? Geez, Dan, do you have a different car for each season?"

"Corvette in the summer. But I'll need something else now. No way is Michelle going in that one."

"Big boys, big toys," she murmured. "I guess I'm not in Kansas anymore."

Dan chuckled, but pointed ahead. "Nope, instead you're crawling up the I-93 ramp."

"Slow is good, Danny-boy. Slow-in-snow, that's what I say."

She was babbling. He recognized the signs and couldn't blame her, as the snow continued to accumulate on the road and on the wind-shield, where the wipers were moving at full speed. She might never have been caught on the roads in the middle of a winter storm before.

He glanced, as usual, into the rearview mirror and almost lost his grip. "What the f…? That guy's crazy!"

"What guy? Where?"

"Behind us."

Ally twisted in her seat while he checked the mirror again. The pair of headlights behind him wandered from the left lane to the right, weaving wide and narrow across the highway and back again. Vehicles were maneuvering to stay far behind the jerk—or trying to—but Dan and a few others were in front of the maniac, not knowing where he'd go next, not knowing if they'd be in his path.

"9-1-1," he said out loud.

He sensed Ally glancing his way, but she kept silent. Smart move. He had to watch the road in front and behind them.

He heard the phone dial, heard the voice on the other end and described their situation and location, while his eyes constantly moved from the rearview mirror to the road ahead. Planning, visualizing, judging distances.

Ally turned around. "She's sleeping."

"Good. Relaxed is best." He glanced up. "Ally! I don't see him."

She twisted her body. "Behind you on the left."

Must be in his blind spot. Dan moved over a lane to the right. Off in the distance came the faint sound of sirens.

"Oh, God. Now he's coming this way," Ally warned.

Where the hell was the next exit already? He'd leave this Russian roulette highway in a nanosecond, if he could.

The other car was moving closer behind them. Right or left? Right or left? A blind choice. Dan moved one lane over to the right again and prayed the guy would go straight.

He almost did. Then the other car swiped Dan's side and spun-out, turning and sliding until it hit the guard rail on the right edge of the highway and stopped. Dan gently turned his wheel to the left and tapped the brakes once. The vehicle caught traction and hugged the road without skidding. Sweet! The antilock brakes performed the way they were meant to.

Dan counted to five and remained calm only until he pulled up in front of the damaged car and stopped. Without a word to Ally, he got out of the SUV, fists clenched, ready to kill.

ALLY FOLLOWED HIM. Sure, she was shaking at the close call, but Michelle was still sleeping, miraculously, and Dan—well, Dan's expression told the story. With his head forward, mouth pressed flat, eyes wide and unblinking, the man was breathing fire and ready to charge. She'd try to prevent him from doing bodily harm and landing in jail.

He was already pulling the other driver's door open when she got there. Easy enough when it hadn't been locked. But the man behind the wheel was leaning back in his seat, seemingly asleep.

"For crying out loud," shouted Dan. "You caused enough trouble, you no-good drunken ass, now get up!"

The car stank like a brewery. Ally stepped next to Dan and peered inside.

"For crying out loud." She echoed Dan's disbelief. "I know this man. From the old neighborhood. A drunk then, and a drunk now. He and Cal, a couple of losers."

The driver's eyes opened. He blinked once, twice.

Stepping in front of Dan, she pounced. "Up to your old tricks again, are you, Mr. Murphy? Drinking and driving until you kill someone?"

The man squinted up at her, looking confused.

"Where…?" Then a split second of recognition. "Is that Cal's daughter? Hmm…hmm…the older one, is it? You know I'd never hurt a fly."

"You can tell it to the cops, Mr. Murphy. From behind bars."

"Why don't you come around anymore? We miss you, darlin'. Your daddy misses you."

She wanted to throw up.

"Ally, the police are here." Dan's warm voice, his arm around her, holding her tight. She clung.

One of Boston's finest walked toward them. Ally watched him closely, discerning the moment he smelled the liquor.

"Seems we have a situation. Step out of the car, please."

"Aw, Officer. This little girl's not pressing charges. I was just celebrating the good holiday with her own father. Indeed I was."

Truth? Lie? It didn't matter.

"We certainly are pressing charges," Dan said. "You almost killed us! And a lot of other people, too."

Ally said. "You're an alcoholic, Mr. Murphy. You destroy lives. And I have no use for people like you." Murphy and Cal were two of a kind, harming everyone around them, including children.

When they got back to the SUV, she felt

Dan's hands on her shoulders. He turned her around and pulled her close. "Ally, Ally. You look so lost, so haunted. Don't look backward, look ahead. Your future is with me, and I am *not* an alcoholic. Hear me? I am not Mr. Murphy or Cal. I swear to you on my daughter's life."

He kissed her. Kissed her while the snow-flakes blanketed them in pristine white, muffling the noise of the city.

"Can you take that devastated expression off your face now?" asked Dan. "I promise you, sweetheart, you have not lost your best friend."

SHE CALLED ROZ THE next day. At work, something she always tried to avoid. But her friend sounded cheerful.

"Although I shouldn't be," said Roz. "Holiday times are stressful for clients, so we're busy, but somehow, the staff wants time off, too. So, here I am, the helpful Hanukkah-celebrating coworker, covering for three people all week. Did you have a great Christmas?"

"Yes, I did. In fact, a special Christmas. Until the end. Do you have time to talk for a minute, or should I call you tonight?"

"Uh-uh. It must be important if you called during the day. Shoot."

She filled her friend in on the engagement,

the family and then the car accident. The alcoholic driver.

"Remember, Dan was a drinker when I met him. I know he hasn't touched a drop since, and he's never expressed a desire for it—at least not to me. But he was right. That accident shook me up. Seeing Mr. Murphy brought back all those memories."

"Well, that makes sense. Weird that the driver was someone you knew."

"Should I take that as fate? A warning? I trusted Dan completely behind the wheel yesterday. I trust him with the baby, and I'm starting to trust that he'll survive a game. But now I'm not sure I can believe what he says about himself."

She paused for breath before crying, "He swore on Michelle's life! But I've heard so many lies and empty promises through the years…I just don't know. What if he grabs a beer with the guys? What if he gets drunk again? On the other hand, he's given me no cause to mistrust him. Oh, I hate myself for doubting him now." She sighed. "I want to believe him, Roz. I love that man so much. It's just that seeing Mr. Murphy again…"

A thoughtful silence ensued on the other end of the phone before Roz spoke. "You love him,

Alexis. And I think that's the key to the whole thing. You've spent your entire life being logical. Finding proof. Following rules. And now you're in love, and love isn't logical. It has never been nor will it ever be logical. For anyone. This time, Alexis, you need to follow your heart."

It was an answer she could accept; it actually made sense. And it came from someone she admired and trusted. "I think you're right. I have to follow my heart. I love him, and I won't borrow trouble. Thanks, Roz. I really value your friendship." She disconnected the call and sat quietly for a minute.

Please, Dan. Don't let me down.

THE BOSTON GLOBE—SPORTS
Monday, December 31
HAPPY NEW YEAR, NEW ENGLAND!
PATRIOTS WIN DIVISION TITLE: 15–2
PLAY-OFFS BEGIN
SUPER BOWL FEVER GROWING
The sweet victory against the New York Giants yesterday maintained New England's lead in the Eastern Division of the AFC. Quarterback Dan Delito's near-flawless performance included four touchdown passes in the first half and two in the sec-

ond for a total of 349 yards. "If only my second half was as good as the first," he said later….

"IF ONLY HIS SECOND HALF…" Ally shook her head in disbelief. Was the guy never satisfied? She'd watched the game with his family, everyone agreeing that he'd been unbelievable yesterday. Hot, hot, hot in the cold northeastern winter.

Ally lifted her head from the morning paper when she heard Dan's key in the door. He'd remained in New York overnight this time because of the late game finish.

She ran down the hall and turned the knob. "Welcome home, hero!"

He grinned, kissed her, waved to Louis and closed the door.

"Some hero. I need the hot tub. And I need to stretch every single muscle before they all go on strike."

"Thank goodness the season's almost over," she said.

"Are you kidding, honey? The best part is straight ahead. The race to the big game in Houston is just heating up."

"What are you talking about?"

"We need to get through the divisional play-off game and then the conference championship game first. And then, if all goes well, we'll play in—well, you know, the big one."

"Two more games before it's over?" She heard the dismay in her own voice.

Dan laughed, picked her up and twirled her around the hall. "Hopefully, *three* games before it's really all over. But it's fun, baby. Lots of fun."

And then she remember the conversation with Nicky at the stadium. Dan would go down as one of the greats. The commentators were now comparing him to Dan Marino and Joe Montana. Anything was possible.

"Then you go for it, Danny-boy. You go all the way."

His kiss tantalized her. She was so hungry for more, but he needed the hot tub. She remembered another time in that spa…. Unfortunately, lovemaking would have to wait. She'd do something else for him instead, something loving and supportive for them both.

"I'll take a class," she said. "A football class—if there's such a thing. I'm a good student. I can learn all this stuff."

His shoulders shook, he threw his head back and his mirth filled the house. "So typically Ally," he said, embracing her again. "You'll slice it and dice it until it makes sense and you understand every bit. I love you."

She nestled her head under his chin and against his shoulder, her arms loosely around his waist.

Follow your heart.

She would. Being held by Dan felt so right, she wanted his arms around her forever.

Monday, January 22
SUPER BOWL: BEARS vs. PATS
Boston Globe: CHICAGO CAN'T BEAR OUR MAN DAN
Providence Journal: DARING DAN WILL MAKE BEARS DANCE
New York Post: BEARS vs. PATS = A CONTEST OF GIANTS
Chicago Tribune: BEARING DOWN ON THE PATS

"FUNNY, FUNNY, VERY PUNNY. I like the third one best, though," Alexis said. "Very clever. New York managed to get one of their teams mentioned."

"A Pyrrhic cheer. Neither New York team made it to the end," said Dan.

Ally walked among the newspapers and magazines that were spread all over the floor of the game room. She'd collected two weeks' worth of articles since the Patriots had won the

AFC conference championship last Sunday against the Chiefs after defeating the San Diego Chargers the week before. Tomorrow, Dan and the team would be flying to Houston for a week of publicity and practice before the hoopla next Sunday against the Chicago Bears.

Now, he was reading a book to Michelle as though he hadn't a care in the world. And why shouldn't he, when his daughter's face lit with joy every time she saw him.

"Where's the caterpillar, Michelle?"

Either the baby's little hand happened to touch the hungry caterpillar, or Dan nudged it in the right direction. Regardless, the proud daddy beamed.

"Correct, again! You are so smart, Michelle. And Daddy loves you so much." He kissed her on the belly, causing her to giggle.

Alexis paused among her headlines to look at the other two. They adored each other. Soon, the three of them would be a real family, with all the legal bows tied up nicely. Knocking on Dan's door in October was the best thing she could have done. That autumn day seemed like a lifetime ago, and yet, it also felt like yesterday.

"Time is like a rubber band," she said, "stretching and contracting."

Dan glanced at her, brows raised. When she

explained, he agreed. "When you're unhappy or ill, one day is a hundred years long," he said. "But when you're happy, time flies by. So, I'm guessing you've been happy lately. At least, I'm hoping."

She kneeled on the floor next to him and Michelle, cupped Dan's face and leaned close, her lips touching his. "When did you get so smart?" she whispered.

"Can't let my almost wife outdo me in the brainy department," he joked.

And for a few minutes, they needed no words.

"I love you, Dan Delito," she whispered. "So, please come out whole after the game. Life is more fun when time flies."

"I know what you mean," he replied. "And I'll do my best."

HE'D TAKEN CARE OF PERSONAL responsibilities before leaving—paying bills, checking with Maria and Ally about household matters, reserving a separate suite for the family at the hotel, arranging with Louis to take his folks, Joe, Mary Ann and Ally to the airport—and giving the man a hefty cash gift for all he'd done that season. All the kids, including Michelle, would stay home with Theresa and Larry.

On the chartered jet taking them to Houston,

Dan studied each member of his team, evaluating their strengths and weaknesses against Chicago. It was his fourth trip to the Super Bowl. He'd lost once and didn't want to lose again. Although he'd arrive with more maturity this time, his excitement was just as high as when he played the first time. He glanced at the ring he wore on his left hand now—his first earned ring. That had been a great day.

Kim had been there, of course. His parents, too. The victory had overwhelmed the young Turk he'd been. They'd all partied into the night after the ceremonies and official duties were over.

If they won again next Sunday, he'd wear the new ring. If they didn't win, he wouldn't wear any. In honor of Ally and Michelle, in honor of a new beginning. But he wanted to win. To be the provider. To show Ally she could count on him. His future life beckoned, a future he desired very much.

Time to talk with the coaches and management. He wanted every edge he could get for the team, and if his new idea made him unpopular with the players for a while, so what? They'd love him in the end—when they won.

That night after dinner, the team gathered in a private meeting room. At the appropriate time, Dan stood.

"I'll make this brief. I've done a little research, and I'm instituting a new rule about family visits. There will be none. When our families arrive at the end of this practice week, they will not visit us in our rooms. None of us need kids crying next door while we're studying. I sure don't and neither do you."

Silence greeted him, then some low grumbling.

"I thought Diaper Dan liked babies."

Dan stood his ground, echoing Ally's words. "This is a business trip, gentlemen. The same as other men with families take. What they don't take are their kids."

He leaned on the table in front of him. "We're here to do a job—*the* job. I'm here to win. In order to win, we practice hard with no distractions from family. That might be exactly the little edge we need against a tough competitor like Chicago."

On the field, they'd follow his every call, every movement. They'd protect him in every way they could.

Now, Dan began to sense a similar tension in the air—the hum of possibility.

He slowly looked from one man to the other. "Any more questions?"

One hand went up. "Do you know something we don't?"

"Yeah. I know I want to win."

"And I want to know, where's the victory party?"

The men started to smile. They were all on board now.

ALEXIS CHEERED AS LOUDLY as anyone, but her nerves were shot by the end of the first quarter, even though the Patriots were leading 7–0. Once again, she didn't know how she'd make it through the entire game without falling apart. She tried. She really tried to step back, relax and repeat her new mantra—Dan knows what he's doing, Dan knows what he's doing. It worked for about a minute, then she'd start getting nervous all over again.

She glanced at Dan's family to see them all with grins spread across their faces.

"Ally has the right idea," said Joe with a wink. "Not counting her chickens yet, so she's not cracking a smile."

Smile? She felt nauseous. "I'm just glad he's not hurt." Yet.

"Remember, he's trained for this, Ally, and right now, he's thinking like a winner. In fact, this is one of his best games ever. Right, Dad?"

"They're evenly matched," said Nick.

"And that's too darn bad," Rita countered, a comment with which Alexis agreed.

By the end of the half, the Bears had made a comeback and had taken the lead, 10–7. Joe's belief never wavered, but Ally kept quiet. Each time Dan caught the snap, she stopped breathing, inhaling again only when he successfully passed the ball downfield. When he was sacked in the second quarter, she couldn't breathe at all.

"My stomach's in knots," she said.

"So is mine," said Rita. "Let's get an ice cream."

Ally giggled. "Food. Your answer to everything is food."

"You bet. I can think of worse things."

Ally could, too, but she didn't want to go there today. The past was over.

Thirty minutes later, the teams retook the field. From that moment until the last down, Ally remained in her seat, eyes riveted to Number 8.

The third-quarter play was brutal, with each team providing a gritty defense. No touchdowns scored by either team. The Bears eked out one field goal; the Patriots came up with two, tying the score at 13 when the fourth quarter began. The teams certainly were well-matched, but Ally couldn't appreciate that nuance.

At this point, Ally didn't care who won. She just wanted it over. Around her, she heard Mary Ann talking to Joe, sensed Rita's presence, heard the men's shouts and cheers as though in an echo chamber. She was in her own space, her own world, with Dan.

How, in God's name, could the fourth quarter be tougher than the third? She was afraid to cover her eyes. Afraid not to be there for Dan if something bad happened. As the clock ticked down, neither team ran enough yardage to get close enough for a field-goal attempt. As for a TD, forget about it. Until the very last pass in the very last minute of the game.

Instantly, Ally whirled toward the family. "Did you see that? What he did? Ohmygod! We won!"

CHAPTER THIRTEEN

THE STERLING SILVER Lombardi Trophy seemed to glow in the Houston sunshine. Dan's pulse beat double time as the NFL Commissioner presented the prestigious award to the Patriot's owner right after the game in front of a world-wide audience of over 130 million people.

They'd done it. His team had done it, by a score of 19–13. It had been an exciting game, a hard-fought game where they'd grappled for every yard in the air and on the ground. But in the end, his guys had come through. The defense had done a great job in holding the Bears to thirteen points. The offense had managed the critical touchdown in the last minutes. The fans had gotten into it, and Dan was still in one piece. Ally would be happy.

The trophy ceremony was over, and the commissioner seemed prepared to speak again.

"On behalf of the National Football League,

and the Patriots' management and coaching staff, we would like to present at this time, the MVP Award for the Super Bowl–winning New England Patriots. By unanimous vote, will quarterback Dan Delito step forward?"

Was that his name? Someone pushed him from behind, and then he was at the microphone, shaking hands with all the big shots.

"Say something to the fans, Dan."

The mike was in front of him now. Saying thank-you was a good way to start.

"It was a team effort. A quarterback is nothing without good receivers, and the offense counts on the defense to do their job. The Bears put up a good fight, so winning today is something to be proud of. We all did our jobs well today, so thank you. I loved every minute of it!"

He stepped back, hoping he'd made some sense. The crowd was still cheering, so maybe he had.

Al Tucker shook his hand. Didn't say a word. Then, one by one, they all came, the ones who'd played actively that day and the ones in reserve. Not a lot of words. It didn't matter.

Later, the words came fast and furious in the locker room. So did the traditional Gatorade waterfall over head coach Rick Thompson. A case of chilled champagne was opened, the bottles distributed to every player, and each man imbibed and celebrated. They chatted with sports reporters from all media. Especially Dan Delito. Every writer wanted a piece of him. He answered question after question, quenching his thirst from his bottle as he went along.

In the outside stadium, the locker room activities were shown on the jumbo screens at each end of the field. Most of the fans stayed glued to the indoor action, including Dan's family and Ally.

ALLY STARED SO HARD AT the screen, her eyes burned. Bit by bit, her body became numb—feet, legs, stomach, arms, fingers. A wave of dizziness attacked. Then a chill. Finally, pain sliced through her so sharply, she doubled over in her seat.

Her beautiful world had collapsed right before her eyes.

She should have known! She shouldn't have trusted him. An entire bottle of champagne? The one time, the very first time, she'd given her heart to a man, she'd been betrayed.

Love wasn't logical. But it should be.

She had to get out of Houston, fly home, air out her condo, find a job. Take her life back. She took a big breath and set the dial on her heart to deep-freeze. She'd cry later—if she defrosted again.

After telling Rita she had a headache, Ally made her way to the large suite the family shared and got on the phone. Ten futile minutes later, she was at a loss. Every plane to Boston was booked solid. She'd have to punt. Isn't that what Dan always said?

So, she'd put on a smile, attend the victory party that evening and keep everything nice-nice. She'd had a lot of experience in pretending when she was a kid, a lot of experience in hiding what was going on in her home and in her head. She could do that today.

Tomorrow, however, would be a different story.

TODAY HAD BEEN ONE of the best days of his life, and the evening promised to be even better. Two hours after the game, Dan stepped out of the shower in his own hotel room, shaved and dressed in party casual—slacks and a dress shirt open at the collar.

As usual, every muscle ached despite the massage he'd received from the trainers after the news conference. He popped an ibuprofen and shrugged. When he finally saw Ally, he wouldn't care about an ache or a pain.

He brushed his hair, swished with mouth-wash and examined himself in the mirror. Sat-isfied all was in place, he left to join his family in their suite. To join Ally. Tonight, he'd show her off to his buddies. Introduce her as his fiancée. A perfect event, perfect timing.

Five minutes later, he was surrounded by his folks, his brother and Mary Ann, slaps on the back, lots of noise. Behind them stood Ally.

She stepped toward him in a sexy green cocktail dress, high-heeled sandals and long gold earrings. Heat blasted his body. That woman could turn him on like no one else.

"Congratulations, Dan. You worked hard for this." Without meeting his glance, she pecked him on the cheek. "Oops, got lipstick on you."

Who cared? Something was wrong. Her smile was forced, definitely wasn't reaching her eyes. His good feelings evaporated.

He touched his forehead to hers. "What's the matter, sweetheart?"

She startled, her complexion paled, and he went on alert. He didn't want to play *Gotcha*. Not with this woman.

"Headache," she said, leaning away, rubbing her temple. "I had to come up here to the suite right after the game."

He exhaled with relief. The game had been hard on her. "I've got some generic meds in my pocket. I just took one myself. Here you go."

Her hand was ice-cold when she touched his.

Maybe she had more than a headache, maybe she was sicker than she let on.

"Honey, if you're really not feeling well, you don't have to put yourself through all the hoopla and noise that goes with the show downstairs." He kissed her forehead, and lingered a moment. "Mom used to do that to see if we had a fever. Truthfully, I can't really tell, but if you're sick, you stay here."

So, why did she look like she was going to cry?

"Just give me an hour to lie down, and I'm sure I'll be all right. I'll find you in the ballroom. Go, go, everyone. I'll see you later."

She took her shoes off and lay on the couch in the living room—her assigned bed, he supposed, the two bedrooms being occupied by the couples.

He kneeled on the floor beside her. "There's tight security, so here's your admission ticket to the ballroom." He handed it to her, kissed her again. "I'm so sorry you're feeling bad."

"Not as sorry as I am."

SHE'D EITHER LOST SOME of her acting ability, or she couldn't keep a secret from Dan. That was her conclusion after an hour of thought. Long ago, she could have fooled the world with her pretending skills. Today, she couldn't divert the one person she wanted to. Of course, she loved that one person, which was why she'd fallen apart.

She put on her sexy sandals, refreshed her lipstick and headed out the door, ID in hand. She'd go to this shindig, her last hurrah with Dan. He deserved this honor, and he deserved her cooperation, at the very least.

As soon as she entered the crowded room, he was beside her, his face alight as if he'd glimpsed his personal heaven.

"I was watching for you. Feeling better?"

"Good enough to help you celebrate."

In the crowd of football players and their families, she was able to paste on her smile and keep it there. From one group to another, Dan led her around, sometimes introducing her as "the best touchdown he'd ever made."

"So, when's the big day?" asked his friend, Al Tucker.

"You'll be the first to know," laughed Dan. "We're not quite there yet."

"Lots of things have happened recently," said Ally. "We're still catching our breaths."

The good wishes continued throughout the evening. Even on the dance floor, people waved cheerfully at them, filling Ally with pleasure and pain. But for Dan it was all pleasure. A perfect evening. She saw to that.

Just as her mother would have done for Cal.

She tripped midstep. Where had that idea come from? She would never, ever become an enabler like Peggy. She'd promised herself a million times to do everything exactly the opposite way her parents had.

"Easy, baby. Headache back?"

Not the kind he thought.

"Just clumsy." She smiled up at him, and that's all it took for him to kiss her as if he meant it.

"I love you, Ally, and I can't wait to get home."

"I can't wait, either. We have a lot to do." Like getting on with their separate lives.

"Yup. Exactly." He tightened his embrace, and they danced as though they'd been dancing together for years.

She would remember every touch, every kiss, the comfort of those arms around her, the broad chest and the love shining in his eyes. This was her Cinderella moment with the prince. The story would end later, of course. She'd run away to her condo, remove the strappy sandals and put on her practical pumps again.

They joined his family a few minutes later. Their reserved table was crowded with extras.

"Working the crowd, guys?" asked Dan,

patting his dad and brother on the shoulder while greeting everyone. "Anybody thirsty? I'm going to the bar."

He looked at Ally. "Thirsty, Ally? Want a drink?"

"Yes. Whatever you're having." The words rushed out of her mouth, and she hated herself for setting a trap.

"Be right back," he said, his glance lingering on her for a long moment.

True to his word, he returned quickly, looking like a waiter with a round tray filled with drinks. He distributed the rest, then handed her an ice-cube-filled highball glass of pale amber liquid laced with tiny bubbles. He took an identical one and raised it in a toast.

"Here's to Michelle. May she grow up knowing how to love and trust." Accent on the last word.

Ally almost dropped her glass. Trap him? She was the one caught, a novice manipulator compared to Dan, who was a master at complex plays.

"Amen." She took a sip. Ginger ale. Despite the heat of an embarrassed blush, she met his glance and nodded. *Touché*.

She spent an uncomfortable night on her couch in the family suite. Dan hadn't invited her to his room.

ON THE PLANE BACK TO Boston the next afternoon, Dan kept his eyes closed, feigning sleep. In another few minutes, however, he wouldn't have to pretend. He'd tossed and turned in his lonely bed after last night's festivities, barely able to rest. Ally should have been with him, but he was emotionally scattered—high on victory, but raw with Ally's distrust. Not to mention his need for more ibuprofen. He ached all over, and normal recovery usually took almost two days.

It was better for him and Ally to have separate beds than to blow the conversation they'd need to have. Conversation or confrontation. Disappointment ballooned inside him. He'd thought confrontation in his life was now limited to a grassy field.

From the time he'd showed up at training camp last July, he'd been fighting for a trophy, and since October, he'd been showing off his prowess to Ally. Showing off in all ways. Isn't that what a man in love did? He'd worked hard, provided a home, tried to be a good daddy to an infant. He'd shared ideas and dreams for a wonderful future with Ally. As for lovemaking—well, they didn't have a problem there. Most important, he'd tried to erase her first impression of him and show her that booze was unimportant.

All his efforts meant nothing if a few slugs of

champagne could upend her as they had. It hadn't been hard for him to put two and two together. He knew Ally as well as he knew his playbook. But he couldn't live his life wondering if she'd sack him, too, if she trusted him or not. If he were alone on the plane right now, he'd cry.

At Logan Airport, passengers in the terminal cheered the team. The *Globe*'s photographers were there, too. Dan offered his best smile, waved to the crowd and called out comments. Everyone was riding high on the win. He wished he could have enjoyed it more himself.

In the limo, he focused on Louis, giving the man a play-by-play of the game highlights, which distracted Dan from his personal homecoming. Regardless, it seemed like an eternity until he opened his own front door…and found no one home.

No Ally. No Michelle. Not what he'd expected.

He left his suitcase in the hall and walked toward the kitchen where a light burned. Maybe a note?

Not a note, but a set of keys. For a moment, his brain came to a screeching halt, his mind a blank. Then his thoughts flew faster than light. What was she thinking? Had she been so frightened that she'd moved out with the baby and run back to her apartment? Dammit! He hadn't taken her for a coward.

He took the stairs three at a time while grabbing his cell and auto dialing her number. No ring. His mobile was dead. Damn, but it made sense because he hadn't charged it in over a week. He opened her bedroom door, then her closet door, and sagged with relief. Her clothes were still there. Everything was the same. Including his imagination.

The doorbell chimed, and he lost no time running down the two flights. He pulled the door open so hard, it almost slammed into his face. And there she was. Baby stroller and Michelle, too.

"What happened?" he asked, drawing them inside quickly.

"We went for a walk. I forgot my keys and my gloves. We were locked out. We walked and walked, you know I like to walk, and thank God I had plenty of baby blankets and the windscreen for the stroller, and your stupid cell phone wasn't working. And my hands are freezing."

"Let's get you warmed up." She was right. Her hands felt like ice and looked almost purple. He gently took them in his own and blew on them.

She burst into tears.

"A little frostbite, Ally. I know it hurts."

"Who cares about that?" she said. "Danny, we can't go on like this."

"I know, and we won't. But first things first."

"Michelle! She's too warm. We need to take off the blankets and snowsuit. I can't do it. My stupid hands." Her words ended in a wail of frustration.

"Don't fall apart on me, kiddo. The baby is fine. Look."

In fact, Michelle was gleeful, excited. He lifted her from the stroller, and she snuggled against him in her favorite position right on his shoulder under his chin. Funny. Ally loved that spot, too.

Despite her protestations, he knew Ally's hands hurt, that they felt like pins and needles sticking and throbbing all at once. He'd been in the same position more than a few times in his life. She didn't say a word now, just paced the hallway, hands out in front of her, mouth tight.

"I can only blame myself," she muttered.

"Talking to me?" asked Dan.

She didn't respond, just kept muttering. "Logical Alexis, perfect Alexis. So organized, she forgot the keys, forgot her gloves, put the baby in danger."

"You did not! She's absolutely fine." Maybe Ally had been distracted by other things, like their engagement.

She came over and rubbed her cheek against Michelle's. "Are you fine, sweet petunia? Daddy says you are." She glanced at him. "I think she's okay. I'm still new at this, too."

"We're both still learning, Ally," he said, leading her into the kitchen.

"But I don't want to make a mistake."

He started to laugh. "You've got to be kidding. Honey, that's part of life. That's how you learn. Forget the football class, you should actually play a sport—soccer, volleyball, softball—any one of them will do. If you miss your mark, you do it better next time."

She cocked her head, paused for a moment. "I'd hate all that attention on me. What if it's my fault that the team loses?"

"That's the way it goes," he said with a shrug. "You don't make the same mistake next time. What about every time you're in court trying to win? How do you handle that pressure?"

"Easy. There are rules of procedure. I know them cold. And besides," she added with a gleam in her eye, "I'm so new, I haven't lost a case yet."

Figured. "Your day will come at some point. Now, let's see your hands."

"They feel a little better." She held them up, and he noticed something besides the frostbite.

"Did you lose your ring out there?" he asked, nodding toward the window.

She seemed surprised at the question, but then quietly said, "No, Dan, no. It's very safe. Upstairs in my drawer."

The time had come to lay everything down, and he was taking the lead. "You were right earlier when you said, 'We can't go on like this.'"

"I know," she whispered. "I'm so sorry."

"Forget the apologies. Just answer one question."

She raised her eyes to him and waited.

"What are you doing Wednesday night?"

"Wednesday? You want to wait two days to talk about the champagne and the Super Bowl after party?"

"I do. It's important." He'd wait two years if it would guarantee a successful outcome with Ally.

"Fair warning, Dan. I am not discussing our private lives in a locker room, a restaurant or even an AA meeting."

What was she talking about? And then it hit him. He'd never told her where he went each week. Man, he had screwed up. She continued to stare at him, brow wrinkled, probably still trying to figure out his Wednesday night destination.

"I owe you an apology, Ally," he said. "I didn't mean to keep my whereabouts a secret."

He paused for a moment. "I do go to a meeting," he said carefully, "but it's with my therapist. I sought help because of you."

"A therapist?" she whispered. "You went because of me?"

"I love you, Ally. And when you love someone, you want to do it right." He reached out and touched her cheek. "So, will you come with me?"

SHE WANTED TO MELT against that strong, protective hand, pretend she hadn't seen him drink that damn champagne. But she couldn't pretend. Echoing the lives of her parents was not an option for her. Her disappointment in him was breaking her heart, and she didn't know how she would survive.

Her poor hands started tingling again, but not because of the cold outside. She was afraid inside. Unsettled. He wanted her to go to a therapist with him, but if she went, a professional might ask *her* a few questions. She didn't want that. She had nothing she wanted to say.

On the other hand, she'd already made her decision to break their engagement, so she had nothing more to lose by going with him. Logical conclusion.

"All right," she said slowly. "I'll go." Above

all else, the man deserved her support for taking such a dramatic step to overcome his problem.

"Thank you."

"But I won't wear the ring, Dan, because I can't keep the promise it represents, not anymore."

She saw the pain in his eyes, the hurt, the shadows. But all he did was nod. "I understand. You have to be true to yourself."

Two evenings later, they left Michelle at home with a delighted Maria and headed toward the office of Dr. Marjorie Tanner, a behavioral psychologist specializing in addictions. They hadn't discussed the ring again.

Dan reached over and squeezed Ally's hands, which were folded in her lap like a schoolgirl's.

"Look at you!" he laughed. "You're not going to the guillotine. Relax. The doc's a nice lady."

He was probably right about the therapist, so what was Ally so afraid of? The discussions would be all about Dan, not about her.

She leaned back, stretched her arms out in front of her and took a deep breath. "I'm sure she is. I'm just an idiot."

"Never that."

The four-story building of psychiatric specialties was affiliated with one of Boston's leading medical institutions. Dan knew his way around, from parking garage to evening access to the place.

"I would have gotten lost here," Ally said.

"I never missed an appointment."

Message received. He was dedicated to exploring his behavior and wanted her to know it.

Dan was right about the doc. Marjorie Tanner was a nice lady with salt-and-pepper hair, a cordial handshake and a warm smile. She led them to a conversational area of her office boasting club chairs and a sofa and table.

"Dan called to say you'd be along this evening, Ms. Brown, so I'm delighted to meet you before we conclude his sessions."

A curveball. Ally cocked her head toward Dan. "Conclude? You never mentioned that."

"Well, I'm not throwing away Dr. Tanner's phone number," he joked, "but I'm going to be right up-front here, Ally."

He reached for her hand. "Alcohol is your hot button. It's so hot, it scorches both of us. So I thought Dr. Tanner should be the one to explain the reason I can end these sessions now."

She needed time to absorb this idea and remained silent.

The therapist spoke. "Dan, have you considered that Alexis might *prefer* to hear from you?"

"No. She doesn't trust me."

"Of course I trust you," Ally interrupted.

"Not about this," said Dan. "Let's face it. A few sips of champagne after winning the Super Bowl—the Super Bowl!—became the eight-hundred-pound gorilla between us."

He was right, and now they were confronting that gorilla. "But don't you see, Danny? Once you fall off the wagon," she whispered, "life will be just horrible. And I'm not going back there. No, no, no. I'll never go back to *that.*"

His expression softened. "What happened in your house when Cal drank?"

Like a spark to dry wood, his question ignited her. Unwanted memories flooded her. Suddenly, it didn't matter where she was or who was with her. She jumped from the chair and exploded.

"What the hell do you think happened, Dan? Did you think Cal threw me birthday parties, called me beautiful and smart and the best daughter a man could have? Did you think he was kind and loving and protective like you are with Michelle? Pu-leeze, give me a break. Don't you get it yet?"

"Yeah, I get it," he replied, starting to rise, but then sitting back in his chair. "Now you get this. I am not your father. I was never like him, and I will never be like him. You can take that to the bank and deposit it. That is my word."

God, he was angry, but not yelling, not wild like Cal, not in her face. Instead, his voice was direct, so firm and direct—it demanded attention.

She listened.

"Am I a drunk, Ally? Have I been drinking? The disease doesn't even run in my family! Think back. Did I slobber at the party in Houston?"

"Well, no. But that doesn't mean you won't."

"I won't because I'm not an alcoholic. Sure, I've abused the stuff now and then in the past, but I'm not addicted."

Psychobabble and gobbledygook. "Prove it, Danny-boy. I saw you drunk the first day we met. I couldn't get near you because you stank so bad. And don't forget the time your brother drank his beer in a cold backyard so you wouldn't be tempted to have one. He's known you longer than I have, and he was concerned."

"You saw me on a day I couldn't handle grief. I was depressed, and I was self-medicating."

"Just another excuse. Believe me, I've heard them all."

He glanced at the therapist. "You want to step in here, Doc?"

"Sure," she said calmly, as though she had nothing better to do, "because I can give Alexis some information she might not know."

Ally could deal with information. As Dan

would say, she was used to slicing and dicing facts. Analyzing them.

"A percentage of people abuse alcohol, and don't get better—that is, they don't stop drinking—even when they attend a twelve-step program or keep appointments with a therapist."

"Because they're faking it," Ally pronounced. "They're just going through the motions, and they don't follow through when the meetings are over." She was on firm ground again, thinking of Cal.

"Nope," said the doc with a shake of her head. "These people don't improve because they're not getting treated for their real problem, the one that haunts them deep inside. The one they're trying to forget."

"Such as?" prompted Ally, interested despite her doubts.

"Such as soldiers with post-traumatic stress after combat or victims of child abuse—physical abuse, sexual abuse. Many grew up in alcoholic families, for example."

Images floated in Ally's head again, images she'd always managed to bury. Now, they pricked at the edges of her conscious mind, making her wince, making her body tremble. *Don't tell.* She slapped her hand over her mouth. *Sh-u-sh.*

"Those issues from childhood are the true culprits," the doctor continued. "The alcohol dulls the pain, covers it up."

"But only for a while," said Ally, slowly placing her hand in her lap again. "And then they need more, I guess?"

Tanner nodded. "So it goes on until someone treating them recognizes the confusion. They're abusing liquor but they are not alcoholics."

Dan jumped into the discussion. "I knew what I was doing, Ally, every damn time I got blitzed. And I sure scared the hell out of my family. I should have found Dr. Tanner a year ago. But I told myself that everyone grieves in different ways."

"Which is true," said the therapist.

"Except, I didn't recover," Dan added.

Ally's first instincts had been right. He loved his wife more than he could ever love anyone else. His grief encompassed him. Her throat began to hurt as she tried to be stoic.

"Ally! Sweetheart. I'm not trying to hurt you. I'm only trying to explain. And here's the critical part. While I was grieving for Kim, there was something else, too. Something I was trying to cover up. And that something else was the issue killing me."

He'd gotten her complete attention. Not just by what he said, but by how he looked. Red-faced, staring at the floor, he actually seemed ashamed.

"What, Dan?" she asked, kneeling next to him. "What could have upset you more than losing her?"

He barely met her glance. "In the end, I let her die alone. I was some husband. Some lousy husband. I wasn't there. I was in Tampa, throwing a football like a madman. Her caregiver had left the room for a few minutes, and Kim just…just passed away. All alone."

Guilt. His grief might have eased naturally except for the guilt. He was a sensitive man, one of the qualities Ally so appreciated. She squeezed his hand, hating to see him at his wit's end.

"I've read that the dying often wait to be by themselves. They need the freedom to go, with nobody holding them back."

"True," Dr. Tanner said.

"The guilt ate me up," he said, "and every so often, like during the week of my anniversary, I tried to ease that pain with Jack Daniel's. After I met you, I realized I needed help dealing with it, so I found Dr. Tanner."

"After you met me?" she whispered. "Because of the baby? Because of your new responsibilities?"

"No," he replied, looking at her then, his dark eyes as black as eternity. "Because of you. I fell in love with you, Alexis Brown, and I don't want to lose you over a glass of champagne."

THE MAN HAD JUST emptied his heart and exposed his most personal secrets for her examination. He had brought her to Dr. Tanner, whom he trusted and whose code of ethics matched Ally's.

Dan had put everything on the line. For her.

He deserved better than Alexis Brown.

She was a coward. All her life, she'd been running from her past by chasing after two goals—education and career. But she'd never had the courage to want more. To expect more. To open herself up to love and go after it. She'd brushed that idea aside and never pictured herself with a richer, fuller life, a life with friends and a family of her own.

She'd never had the courage to find out why.

Until today. Until right now.

She had remained kneeling next to Dan's chair, his hand still in hers. Staring at the wall behind him, she whispered, "Dan, I'm scared."

"Oh, Ally." The disappointment in his voice was palpable.

"No, no. I'm sorry. You misunderstood. I'm

not scared of you. Just…" She squeezed his hand tightly, and whispered, "Hold my hand, too?"

"Absolutely."

Warmth. His hands were warm around hers. As always. Steady and supportive. As always. She glanced up at the woman who'd remained quietly watching.

Tell her. Tell her. Tell her! "What you said before—" *Breathe, breathe.* "About child abuse. My father… he—he drank a lot. He hit a lot. And one night when I was fourteen, he was drunk and he said I was a woman…and he caught me and dragged me to the couch… and…and…I fought him…I tried…"

She remembered every detail and gulped for air, her chest so tight she was panting, but she had to finish the story while she could.

"But I couldn't get away…and then he raped me and I was crying and *'please, please, please'*…and—and my mother—my mother! She just watched! That's all she did…and I don't know how could she do that." Sobbing, she squinted at the doctor and cried, "How… how could she do that to me?"

She was done. Out of words, her voice trailed away, her body as limp as the rag doll Sherri used to play with, the one she carried with her at all times, the one she named Michelle.

Alexis barely knew where she was.

"Easy, baby, easy," Dan's low voice rumbled in her ear. "I'm right beside you."

Thank goodness.

Then he leaned over and scooped her onto his lap.

Even better.

She wondered why he wasn't disgusted, why he could still touch her.

"I thought I left the chaos behind me when I left that house," she said, surprised she wanted to reveal more, "but I guess I didn't. And my poor little sister, Sherri…she was alone with them. I left her there alone, the day I graduated high school and walked out. I'll never forgive myself."

She paused then, exhausted, as her tears rolled, but she still hadn't finished. "It seems I brought all the secrets, all the unhappiness, right along with me into adulthood, didn't I, Dr. Tanner?"

"You're facing it now, and it's never too late."

"It's affecting my life, and Dan's, and I don't want that. You heard him yourself. Alcoholism doesn't run in his family, but it sure runs in mine. It is my hot button, like he said. I always assume everyone drinks like Cal. I condemn everyone before I know the truth. I'm even suspicious of a glass of wine. I don't trust anyone about this." She struggled for another breath.

"And I don't want to live that way anymore. Can you help me?"

"Absolutely. You've already made a great start." The woman walked to her computer. "I seem to have an opening on Wednesday evenings," she said with a smile. "How does that sound?"

"Totally frightening, but absolutely fine. I'll be here."

"Just think of it as a practice session," Dan said. "You're the quarterback and the doc's the coach. It's a snap."

The other two groaned in unison, wry smiles following. "A little humor is always good medicine," said Dr. Tanner. "But Dan, try to up the game, will you?"

Groaning and chuckling again, Ally left the office with Dan, walking arm in arm. A thoughtful silence surrounded them, lasting until they entered the car. As Dan was about to press the ignition, Ally stopped him.

"Before we go home…" She turned toward him, her gaze darting everywhere except at Dan. She twisted strands of hair through her fingers. More than anything else, she wanted to hide her face. The shame of it. What Cal did was beyond horrible. It was criminal, in all ways. She had to clear the air. She tried to find the words.

Dan beat her to it.

"It wasn't your fault, Ally. None of it. In fact, I'd like to pay your old man a visit he'd never forget." He leaned down and kissed her until her doubts fled.

"About my appointments with Dr. Tanner…"

"You're going. I'll drive you there myself and wait in the car."

"I'm—I'm not used to discussing these things."

"An understatement," he interrupted with a gentle smile. "But as the doc said, you made a great start tonight."

"I'm scared. I hate him. I hate the man. And now I'll have to talk about him." Her tears ran then, silent tears from a hurt so deep, it had never had a voice until now.

"I was scared, too, Ally, but I didn't want to lose you. My love for you was stronger than my fear, so I made the appointment. I will admit that talking was hard in the beginning. But I learned a lot.

"I want you to remember this—you and I are in this life together. All the way. We don't run just because we get sacked a few times."

She stretched closer to him until she could cover his mouth with hers. "You are the most amazing man I've ever met," she said, punctuating her words with kisses. "The smartest. The most loving man, too."

"Say that when I'm not behind the wheel of a car," he teased, "and I can do something about it."

She glanced at her watch. "Hmm…maybe in an hour or so."

"It's a date," he replied. "And by the way, you forgot something back at the house. It's in my pocket."

She reached inside his jacket and felt the small box. Without another word, she put her ring back where it belonged.

EPILOGUE

THE BOSTON GLOBE—SOCIETY
Sunday, July 22
MS. ALEXIS BROWN WEDS QUARTER-
BACK DANIEL NICHOLAS DELITO
Ms. Alexis Brown and Mr. Daniel
Nicholas Delito were united in marriage on
July 21st at 11 o'clock in the morning at
St. Mary's Catholic Church in the north
end. A reception immediately followed at
Gillette Stadium in Foxborough.

The bride, wearing a silk shawl over a
strapless, classically styled Vera Wang
white silk gown with delicate white and
silver embroidery, was escorted to the altar
by Mr. Joseph Delito, who was also best
man to his brother.

The four flower girls, led by one-year-
old Michelle Delito, daughter of the
groom, included Misses Elizabeth, Emily

and Grace Newman, nieces of the groom. Miss Michelle toddled down the aisle carrying a bottle of milk in one hand and rose petals in the other.

Hometown hero Dan Delito's career spans eight years with the New England Patriots, seven of those as starting QB with three Lombardi Trophies to his credit. Ms. Brown worked as a prosecutor for the District Attorney's Office before gaining custody of her niece, Michelle Delito.

The young family will take up residence in suburban Brookline before the new football season begins.

* * * * *

Rancher Ramsey Westmoreland's temporary cook is way too attractive for his liking. Little does he know Chloe Burton came to his ranch with another agenda entirely....

That man across the street had to be, without a doubt, the most handsome man she'd ever seen.

Chloe Burton's pulse beat rhythmically as he stopped to talk to another man in front of a feed store. He was tall, dark and every inch of sexy—from his Stetson to the well-worn leather boots on his feet. And from the way his jeans and Western shirt fit his broad muscular shoulders, it was quite obvious he had everything it took to separate the men from the boys. The combination was enough to corrupt any woman's mind and had her weakening even from a distance. Her body felt flushed. It was hot. Unsettled.

Over the past year the only male who had gotten her time and attention had been the e-mail. That was simply pathetic, especially since now she was practically drooling simply at the sight of a man. Even his stance—both hands in his jeans pockets, legs braced apart, was a pose she would carry to her dreams.

And he was smiling, evidently enjoying the conversation being exchanged. He had dimples, incredibly sexy dimples in not one but both cheeks.

"What are you staring at, Clo?"

Chloe nearly jumped. She'd forgotten she had a lunch date. She glanced over the table at her best friend from college, Lucia Conyers.

"Take a look at that man across the street in the blue shirt, Lucia. Will he not be perfect for Denver's first issue of *Simply Irresistible* or what?" Chloe asked with so much excitement she almost couldn't stand it.

She was the owner of *Simply Irresistible*, a magazine for today's up-and-coming woman. Their once-a-year Irresistible Man cover, which highlighted a man the magazine felt deserved the honor, had increased sales enough for Chloe to open a Denver office.

When Lucia didn't say anything but kept staring, Chloe's smile widened. "Well?"

Lucia glanced across the booth at her. "Since you asked, I'll tell you what I see. One of the Westmorelands—Ramsey Westmoreland. And yes, he'd be perfect for the cover, but he won't do it."

Chloe raised a brow. "He'd get paid for his services, of course."

Lucia laughed and shook her head. "Getting paid won't be the issue, Clo—Ramsey is one of the wealthiest sheep ranchers in this part of Colorado. But everyone knows what a private person he is. Trust me—he won't do it."

Chloe couldn't help but smile. The man was the epitome of what she was looking for in a magazine cover and she was determined that whatever it took, he would be it.

"Umm, I don't like that look on your face, Chloe. I've seen it before and know exactly what it means."

She watched as Ramsey Westmoreland entered the store with a swagger that made her almost breathless. She *would* be seeing him again.

Look for Silhouette Desire's
HOT WESTMORELAND NIGHTS
by Brenda Jackson,
available March 9 wherever books are sold.

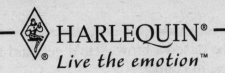

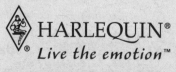

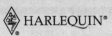

Invites *you* to experience lively, heartwarming all-American romances

Every month, we bring you four strong, sexy men, and four women who know what they want—and go all out to get it.

From small towns to big cities, experience a sense of adventure, romance and family spirit—the all-American way!

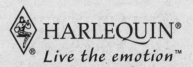

Love, Home & Happiness

HARLEQUIN®
INTRIGUE®

BREATHTAKING ROMANTIC SUSPENSE

Shared dangers and passions lead to electrifying romance and heart-stopping suspense!

Every month, you'll meet six new heroes who are guaranteed to make your spine tingle and your pulse pound. With them you'll enter into the exciting world of Harlequin Intrigue— where your life is on the line and so is your heart!

THAT'S INTRIGUE— ROMANTIC SUSPENSE AT ITS BEST!

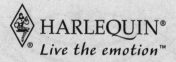

Harlequin® Historical
Historical Romantic Adventure!

*Imagine a time of chivalrous
knights and unconventional ladies,
roguish rakes and impetuous
heiresses, rugged cowboys
and spirited frontierswomen—
these rich and vivid tales will
capture your imagination!*

*Harlequin Historical . . .
they're too good to miss!*

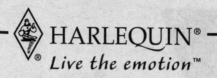

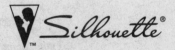